New England Rocks

Christina Courtenay

Copyright © 2013 Christina Courtenay

Published 2013 by Choc Lit Limited

Penrose House, Crawley Drive, Camberley, Surrey GU15 2AB, UK
www.choclitpublishing.com

The right of Christina Courtenay to be identified as the Author of this Work
has been asserted by her in accordance with the Copyright, Designs and
Patents Act 1988

A CIP catalogue record for this book is available
from the British Library

ISBN 978-1-78189-030-1

MIX
Paper from
responsible sources
FSC
www.fsc.org **FSC® C020471**

Printed and bound by CPI Group (UK) Ltd, Croydon, CR0 4YY

To my niece Alydia Tapper
and
my nephews Anthony Tapper and Oliver Fenton
with love

Acknowledgements

A couple of years ago I went to a high school reunion to meet up with people I attended the American School in Japan (ASIJ) in Tokyo with during three of my high school years (sophomore to senior). This got me thinking back to that time and although we had great fun, I realised I really wanted to write a book about the sort of thing I would have liked to happen to me back then, rather than what actually occurred. Wishful thinking, daydreaming – call it what you want, but that's what *New England Rocks* was for me. So I'd like to thank all of my fellow ASIJ'ers for inspiring me to write this!

As always, grateful thanks to the lovely Choc Lit team who work their magic on all my stories, and especially my 'American advisor' (you know who you are) for helping me capture our cultural differences – we really are divided by a common language!

And thank you to my friends and family for support and encouragement every step of the way!

Prologue

Rain Mackenzie became aware of the angry voices long before she opened her eyes. They buzzed in and out of her consciousness like wasps, stinging her with their murmured accusations, which she couldn't quite understand. She wanted to shout at them to shut up because the shrill tones were hurting her head. Stabbing it like a knife, in fact, every blow more painful than the last. She couldn't remember ever having a headache this bad before and she wished she could just sink back into oblivion again.

Deciding to do just that, she sighed and snuggled up to the warm body next to her. It felt solid and comforting and she could hear a heartbeat that was soothing to her poor head. She was just about to drift off to sleep again when a disturbing thought hit her, ruining any chance of a rest. *Body? What body?*

Come to think of it, why did the room smell like a distillery? The alcohol fumes suddenly made her gag and she drew in a sharp breath.

'It's an outrage! It simply can *not* be tolerated. She'll have to go. They'll both have to leave, although I would put the blame squarely on the Mackenzie girl myself.'

Rain's fuzzy brain vaguely registered her own name and she frowned. But it wasn't until she finally blinked her eyelids open a fraction that she saw there was a virtual sea of faces staring down at her with accusing glares. One belonged to the headmaster of Blakeborough, the English boarding school Rain was attending, and one to her form tutor, Miss Dalrymple. She couldn't make out the others because the light was too bright. With a groan she attempted to sit up. She swayed with dizziness and put up her hands to hold onto her head in order to stop the world from spinning.

'Ah, about time too.' Miss Dalrymple took a step forward. 'If you're awake, you can come with me this instant, young lady.'

'What?' The word came out as a hoarse whisper because Rain's mouth was drier than the Kalahari Desert. She tried to swallow down the foul taste on her tongue, but that made her feel more nauseous. Fighting the queasiness with another deep breath, she blinked again. *What the hell is going on?*

'Get up, do.' Miss Dalrymple grabbed Rain's arm roughly and attempted to pull her out of bed. 'Thank the Lord you're wearing *something* at least,' she muttered.

Rain looked down at her PJs – regulation knee-length cotton trousers and the short-sleeved top buttoned up securely at the front. Why wouldn't she be wearing it? she wondered. 'But what …?' she started to protest, but the form tutor interrupted her.

'Come away now and leave that poor boy to sleep it off. It will be hours before he surfaces, I shouldn't wonder. It's a miracle you didn't both get alcohol poisoning.' Miss Dalrymple nodded in the direction of a nearby table, where four empty tequila bottles stood in mute witness to what had happened the night before.

Of course, the tequila! Rain had a light bulb moment. No wonder her head was fit to burst. She shuddered as she remembered the strong alcohol mixed with lime and salt, hitting her stomach with fiery power over and over again. She stared at the bottles. She was sure she hadn't drunk all that by herself. *Four bottles? No way.* Besides, there had been other people there too. She remembered her room mate Annabelle, for one, and Rupert and Alastair and who else?

'Milo.' She said the word out loud and finally turned to stare at the body that lay next to her. He wasn't a pretty sight this morning, lying on his back, snoring with his mouth open, dead to the world. She suddenly wondered why she had fancied him rotten the night before. It must have been the tequila that had addled her brain, because there was nothing appealing about him now.

'*Urgh*,' she muttered and turned away, making a face.

Then another unwelcome thought hit her. She and Milo had been sharing a bed, all night, and it wasn't even hers. It was his. She was in the boy's dormitory, which was strictly off limits, and she was only wearing her PJs. *Oh, shit!*

She was in serious trouble.

Chapter One

Just over a week later, Rain found herself outside the local high school in Northbrooke, a tiny New England town a couple of hours north of Boston in the United States. Since this was where her parents currently lived, attending this lowly establishment was to be her punishment for getting herself expelled from Blakeborough. Judging by the exterior, a punishment it would surely be, she thought.

'Why can't you just find me another boarding school?' she had demanded of her father, Sir Anthony Mackenzie, when he told her she was moving. It wasn't as if he couldn't afford it – he was director of a UK banking corporation and currently working in Boston, but even if he hadn't been earning a massive salary that way, he'd inherited a fortune at an early age. Money had never been an issue. 'I'm sorry for what happened, but it was just a prank that got a bit out of hand and you're paying them like squillions each term. Surely they can overlook what I've done and give me another chance?'

'Possibly, but here's the rub,' he'd replied. 'I'm not prepared to shell out "squillions", as you put it, on your education if you're not going to take it seriously. This wasn't the first time the headmaster has had cause to complain of your behaviour. I'm becoming rather bored with hearing about your exploits, you know. The fact is you had your chance and you blew it, basically. Now you have to accept the consequences of your actions.'

Rain thought he was being unnecessarily harsh and hoped to change his mind soon, but in the meantime, this was where she had to stay. Purgatory, by the look of it.

Northbrooke High couldn't have been more different

from Blakeborough if it had tried. Where her former school consisted of a collection of beautiful old red brick buildings in the classical style, this one was all modern, squat and, in her opinion, dead ugly. She sighed and stomped off in the direction of the entrance. After all, it made no difference what it looked like.

There were hordes of teenagers everywhere – in the parking lot, on the front steps and inside the building – but she totally ignored them even though everyone seemed to be staring at her. She had no intention of talking to any of them. *What's the point?* She wasn't planning on staying long. Besides, she didn't want any friends. Not if they were going to behave the way her so-called friends at Blakeborough had. *Selfish bunch of tossers who* … She balled her fists and stopped the thought right there. She refused to even think about them now.

Just inside the main doors, she bumped into someone coming the other way. She raised her eyes to glare at whoever it was, but blinked instead when she realised she'd collided with one of the hottest guys she'd ever seen.

'Whoa, take it easy, babe.' He put out a hand to steady her, but she shook it off.

Straight black hair, fashionably spiky, above intense blue eyes. Chiselled cheekbones and jaw, perfect nose and mouth, and an eyebrow piercing. Rain was a sucker for those. *Yep, seriously fit.* She almost gasped, especially since she had bounced off his substantial chest. She looked up at him, noticing how big he was at close quarters. Not just tall, but broad-shouldered with nicely defined biceps and arms that were covered in dragon tattoos all the way down to his wrists. The sleeveless T-shirt he wore showed these off to perfection and she couldn't seem to drag her gaze away.

'Like what you see?' he asked in a lazy voice, his blue eyes twinkling with teasing laughter when she looked up again.

'No,' she said curtly, but felt herself blush, which made her furious. He chuckled and she knew he probably hadn't been fooled. She *had* liked what she'd seen, very much so, and she wished it wasn't so obvious. *Damn him*, she thought. He must get that reaction all the time. Well, too bad, she wasn't going to fall for him, wicked blue eyes or not. She wasn't falling for anyone ever again.

He seemed to like what he was looking at too and she had to swallow a curse of outrage when she saw the direction of his gaze. He was so tall he could see straight down her top to her lacy lilac bra, as his next words confirmed. 'Purple, huh?' he commented with raised eyebrows. 'Nice.'

'It's lilac, actually, not that it's any of your business.' She swept past him with her head held high and made a mental note not to wear such low cut tops in future. At five foot ten, she was usually on the same level as most boys, but she'd obviously have to be more careful around this guy. He had to be six foot two at the very least, so even with heels on, she was shorter than him.

'Whatever,' she muttered, annoyed with herself for even caring. What did it matter? She wasn't staying long and their paths probably wouldn't cross much in any case.

Finding her way round Northbrooke High didn't prove too difficult and Rain was soon standing before the principal's secretary. She'd entered the room without knocking and waited with arms crossed until the woman stopped talking on the phone to someone.

'Yes, can I help you?' The woman's expression was wary.

'I'm Rain Mackenzie. Apparently I'm starting at this school today.' Rain didn't bother to hide her annoyance. She couldn't care less what anyone here thought. If she wasn't going to sit her A-level exams in the UK this year, she'd have to go back to do them at a crammer school or something. So whatever she did or didn't do here was irrelevant. In fact, she could go the whole year without doing any homework whatsoever because she'd have to do it all again next year. That made her feel even angrier than before. *What a bloody waste of time!*

'Ah, yes, your father rang me on Friday, right?'

Rain nodded.

'Just hang on a sec and I'll see if Dr A has time to see you.'

'Dr A?'

'That's right, *Dr* Allburn, the principal. He has a PhD in child psychology, you know.'

Rain rolled her eyes. *Like I care?*

'Wait here, please.' The woman went to knock on the door to an inner office and disappeared for a short while, then came back. 'Okay, you can go in now.'

Rain wasn't sure what she'd expected, but Dr Allburn certainly didn't fit her image of a principal. The ones she'd had in England had either been of the stern old lady type or doddery professor lookalikes, all of them with distinguished features and an air of dusty academics. Dr Allburn was nothing like that. He was tall and built like a brick wall, and deeply suntanned with a wide smile of impossibly white teeth. His thick hair, although slicked back neatly from his face, was tied into a small ponytail at the back. Rain tried not to stare.

'Hi there, welcome to Northbrooke High.' He had a booming voice that suited his large frame and he shook her hand vigorously. 'I'm Dr Allburn, but the kids all call me Dr A so I hope you will too. Have a seat, please.'

Slightly shell-shocked, Rain sat on the chair he indicated while he seated himself behind his huge desk and smiled at her again. 'So, you've come to join us for a while, huh?'

'Looks that way,' Rain said. *Talk about stating the obvious.*

He grinned. 'I understand this is your first time in the US.'

'Yes, yes it is. My parents only just moved over here.'

'Well, it's not so different to the UK. You'll soon catch on, don't you worry about that.'

'I'm not worried at all, and just so you know, I'm not here of my own free will.'

'Right. Good to get that point cleared up.' She narrowed her eyes at him, not sure if he was making fun of her or not, but he continued blandly. 'So I hear you had a small problem back at your boarding school. That right?'

She snorted. 'You could say that. I don't know what Dad told you, but whatever it was, it's not true. Well, the tequila part is, but not the rest. And I was so not the ringleader, or any kind of leader, and it wasn't my idea, no matter what that ratbag Milo told everyone. He's just a scaredy-cat little shit who's afraid of his dad and blamed it all on me. Very convenient.'

'Hey, hey!' Dr A held up his hands as if to stop her torrent of words. 'We don't blame anyone here for any past misdemeanours, so keep your hat on, okay? You'll be judged on what you do from now on, maybe you could keep that in mind.'

Rain shrugged. She had no intention of doing anything much here at all, but he didn't need to know that right now.

'I'd better get someone to show you around and —'

'That's not necessary,' Rain cut in rudely. 'I can find my own way, thanks. If you just give me my locker number and a class list, I'll take it from there.'

'Ooh-kaaay.' He drew out the word as if he was thinking about it. 'What classes are you taking?'

'How should I know? Whatever I have to, I guess.'

'Well, you're in the Senior year so you can pretty much choose for yourself.' He handed over a piece of paper. 'Here's a list of subjects. You'll have to do one English course of some sort and a math one, but other than that, it's up to you. Minimum six subjects.'

Rain studied the list and quickly made her choices. *This is going to be a doddle.* 'Fine. I'll do Futuristic Literature for English ...' *Futuristic Lit?* She almost laughed as such a subject would never have been taught at Blakeborough, only boring old classics. The list said it consisted of reading sci-fi books and writing a few reports on them, so that should be easy. *That's what I read for fun!* '... uhm, geometry for math ...' She'd done that before, so that would be easy too. '... French and Spanish ...' She was fairly fluent in both from the many holidays spent in the South of France and the Costa Blanca with her parents. '... typing ...' *Typing? Doesn't everyone know how to do that these days?* '... and maybe Home Ed? Is that, like, cooking?'

'Sure is, honey.'

'That's it, then.'

'Great. If you go back out to Mrs Langan and tell her your choices, she'll draw up a schedule for you and you can head straight to your homeroom.'

'Homeroom?'

'First class of the day starts with roll call, announcements, that sort of thing. Doesn't take long.'

Rain stood up and turned for the door. She knew she was being impolite, but she didn't care. Dr A might be a nice man, but she still didn't want to be at his poncey old school, so she didn't give a toss what he thought of her. Just as she reached for the handle, however, he spoke again.

'Oh, I almost forgot. We have a new policy this year – all the Seniors have to participate in an extracurricular activity after school, like team sports or helping out with the Yearbook and stuff. Your choice again, here's a list.' He held out another piece of paper and she walked over to take it reluctantly.

Great, so now I'll be forced to spend even more time in this place every day. Just what she needed. 'Whatever. I'll do football,' she said, after a cursory glance at the sheet.

'Huh? No, that's too violent for girls. You could get seriously hurt.' His eyebrows had risen halfway to his hairline, which looked kind of comical, but Rain suppressed the smile she almost gave him. She didn't want to smile. Not now. Maybe not ever.

'No, I mean football as in soccer.' Rain clarified.

'Oh, right, of course, sorry.' He laughed. 'I forgot that's what you guys call it.'

'Good, then I'll do that, like I said.'

'You sure 'bout that? The thing is, we don't have a girls' team this year. There weren't enough of them interested, so you'd have to try out for the boys' one.'

She shrugged again. 'So? I've played before, at Blakeborough. I was better than some of the boys there, plus I run pretty fast. Or is it a problem? I mean, are girls not allowed or something? Because, you know, that's kind of sexist.' Rain crossed her arms over her chest and adopted a challenging stance, ready to fight her corner. If there was one thing she hated, it was when girls weren't allowed to do something the boys were. She'd always been a tomboy and knew she was just as good as any boy at most things.

'No, no, I don't think there are any rules against having girls on the team. I just thought you might like to know, that's all. Don't be upset if the coach doesn't pick you for the team.'

'Well, it doesn't bother me.'

'Fine, you go right ahead, then. Tell Coach Rivers I said it was okay. Practice sessions are Mondays, Wednesdays and Fridays after school, out back on the playing field. You can go try out this afternoon.'

She nodded and headed for the door again. 'Bye,' she said, then added grudgingly, 'Thanks.'

'No problem.' She could almost hear the smile in his voice, but didn't want to see it, so she didn't look at him again.

Chapter Two

Mrs Langan produced a schedule after much faffing around, which made Rain want to jump up and down with impatience. When the woman had finally finished, Rain only just had time to run to the classroom designated as her 'homeroom' and even then, she was the last person to enter because it took her a while to find it. The Futuristic Lit teacher, a man called Mr Aiden according to Rain's timetable, looked up in surprise. Everyone else fell silent and stared at her. Rain swept the room with a disdainful glare, and almost groaned out loud. At the back of the room sat the guy she'd run into earlier.

Oh, great, that figures. He would have to be in this class, she thought, but she refused to let him distract her. Without looking at him again, she walked up to the teacher's desk.

'I'm Rain. I'm just starting today.' She held out her piece of paper to show him and he glanced at it, before smiling politely and pointing at a desk in the front row.

'Right. Welcome, er, Rain, have a seat. I'm just going to check attendance and then we'll have a discussion about the word "grokking" in Robert Heinlein's novel *Stranger in a Strange Land*. Maybe you can just listen for today and I'll give you a copy to read later so you can catch up.'

'That's okay, I've read it,' Rain said. Her older brother, Rob, passed on a lot of his sci-fi books to her as they both enjoyed the genre, and this had been one of them.

'Oh.' He looked surprised. 'Well, that's good. Then perhaps you'd like to start the ball rolling?'

'No, I wouldn't.' Rain frowned at him while snickering broke out behind her. She ignored that and concentrated her gaze on the teacher who seemed a bit disconcerted. *Well, what did he expect? Honestly, do I look like the kind of person who'd want to start a discussion for him on my first day? What is he, thick?*

His smile faded. 'I see. Yeah, okay, I guess I shouldn't throw you in at the deep end. Not fair. I'll come back to you.'

After making everyone say 'yes' or 'here' as he read out the names of the class, he got down to business and pointed to a guy in the front row, obviously one of the class nerds. 'David, give me your comments, please.'

A few of the geeks started a lively discussion on Heinlein's meaning of the word 'grok', making it seem much more complicated than it actually was, but Rain didn't pay any attention. When asked for her opinion again some time later, she just shrugged and said, 'As far as I could make out, he just meant that it was a way of absorbing information deep into your soul and processing it until you understood fully so that you become a part of whatever you're trying to grok.'

'Good, concise way of putting it. Thank you, er, Rain.' The teacher looked relieved that she'd said something sensible, but the way he kept hesitating before her name irritated the hell out of her.

'Is there a problem with my name?' she asked, fixing him with another glare. Cue more giggling from the back of the classroom. She turned around to scowl in that direction too and was momentarily sidetracked by the sight of the gorgeous guy with black hair. He smiled in lazy acknowledgement of her interest and she forced herself not to stare at him. She was so done with fit guys. They were nothing but trouble.

'What? No, n-not at all,' Mr Aiden stammered. 'I mean, it's unusual, to be sure, but I think your parents made an excellent choice in naming you after something so, uhm, evocative as the weather.'

'They didn't. My real name is Reine, r-e-i-n-e' — she rolled

her *r* and pronounced the word with a perfect accent—
'which is French for "queen", but I prefer Rain, as in water.'

'Right. Thank you. I'm glad we've got that straight.' The
teacher took a deep breath and pulled at his tie as it if was a
bit too tight around his windpipe. 'Now let me give you all
your next assignment.' He turned away and began to write
on the blackboard. Rain didn't bother to make a note as it
was only to read to the end of the book, and as she'd told
him, she had already read it.

Jesse Devlin had to struggle not to laugh out loud. He loved
the way the new girl had wrong-footed Mr Aiden and stared
everyone else down. She had guts, that was for sure. And
he liked the way her gaze had swept the room as if she
really was a queen, but then had kind of stumbled when she
caught sight of him, although she'd recovered quickly. She
was really something else.

He surveyed her from behind. She was definitely easy on
the eyes as well – gorgeous blonde hair tumbling down to her
waist and some shorter, messier pieces over her eyes, great
ass, long shapely legs. She had to be five ten at least, if not
taller, but despite that, she was wearing high-heeled boots so
she obviously wasn't self-conscious about her height. That
was unusual. And she definitely wasn't from around here;
she sounded like James Bond. He smiled to himself. *But that
British accent is a hell of a lot sexier when she does it.*

Bored with the discussion about 'grokking', he leaned his
chair back against the wall and continued his assessment as
she half turned to stare out the window. Cute straight nose,
lush mouth with not even a trace of lip gloss. Big eyes with
eyelashes to die for, like she was Bambi or something. All set
in a perfectly shaped face with flawless skin that didn't look as
if it had any help from make-up. In fact, she was quite simply
stunning, but she seemed totally unaware of it. *Amazing.*

Amber was going to spit nails at this unexpected competition. For a nanosecond, that thought made him smile again, because if anyone needed her ego deflated it was Amber, but then his brain mentally kicked him. *What the hell am I thinking?* Amber was his girlfriend and he ought to be upset on her behalf. Actually, he shouldn't even be looking at other girls because he already had the prettiest one in the school. The one everyone else wanted.

Damn!

His eyes strayed to the front of the classroom once more, almost as if they had a will of their own. He told himself that if he hadn't already been going out with Amber, he might have been interested. It would have been a challenge to tame someone like Rain, but he'd have to let some other guy have a go. As it was, he would look, but that was all.

Surely there was no harm in looking?

As long as Amber didn't catch him at it.

At the end of the class, Rain hurried out without making eye contact with any of the other students. She didn't want to make friends and wasn't interested in their petty little intrigues and cliquey goings-on. Instead, she went and found her locker and put the book the teacher had insisted on giving her inside it, together with the rest of her stuff.

She never carried a handbag – couldn't stand the way they always slipped off her shoulder – so instead she had her mobile and her wallet in the pockets of her miniskirt, as well as a few loose coins. She didn't bother to carry make-up with her either. Once she'd put some moisturiser and mascara on in the morning, that was it as far as she was concerned. Although she noticed this was far from the case with a lot of the girls around her, who were busy with their powder compacts and lipsticks. *How nauseating.* Rain wrinkled her nose. She couldn't stand the taste of lipstick.

It was only a short break, so she made her way to the next classroom on her schedule. Just inside the door, she almost walked into the hot guy again. He'd answered to the name Jesse Devlin when Mr Aiden did the roll call, and although Rain told herself she wasn't interested, her mind had registered the information, which was annoying. He gave her a crooked smile.

'Nice work,' he said, obviously referring to the previous lesson. 'Keep it up, old Aiden needs a good stirring now and then.'

'I wasn't trying to amuse the rest of you,' Rain shot back.

He shrugged. 'Whatever.'

She stared after him as he ambled out the door. Jeez, he was insufferable. Why did it always have to be that way with handsome guys? Milo had been just the same, although she'd started to tame him when … *No! I'm not going to think about that, damn it.*

She sat down at the back of the classroom this time and closed her eyes. She really didn't want to interact with these people. The sooner she got expelled from here too, the faster her parents would have to send her back to England. *Now what can I do to annoy the teachers, other than not do my homework …?*

She wasn't left alone for long.

'Hey, gorgeous, need some help to find your way around on the first day? I'd be happy to help.'

Rain opened her eyes and frowned at the speaker, a hunky blond guy who looked like he spent a lot of time in front of a mirror with his hair dryer. He had also seriously overdone it with the aftershave. It rolled off him in waves, making her want to gasp for air. 'And you are?' she asked, although she didn't really want to know.

'Cody Knight.' He smiled what he obviously thought was a 100-watt smile and waited for her reaction. She didn't change her expression in the slightest and had the satisfaction of seeing him frown just a little when this charm offensive failed.

'Well, Cody Knight, thanks for the offer, but I can find my own way round.' She closed her eyes again to show him that the conversation was at an end, but he didn't give up that easily.

'Aw, come on, surely you don't want to eat lunch all by yourself? Let me take you to the cafeteria and introduce you to people.'

She looked at him again and sighed. Out of the corner of her eye, she saw that Jesse had taken a seat on her left. He was obviously listening to this conversation because he was smirking. That made her even more irritated and she shot him a dagger look before answering Cody. 'Thanks, but no thanks. There's no point because I'm not staying long. Wouldn't want anyone to be sad when I leave.'

'What?' Cody was frowning for real now, looking totally confused. Good-looking, but no brain, Rain concluded. He too reminded her of Milo, which wasn't in his favour. Milo was seriously fit but had zero brain capacity, and although Rain had thought at one time that it didn't matter, she knew now she'd never again go out with a complete moron, no matter what he looked like. Looks definitely weren't everything.

'Like I said, I'm only staying here temporarily, so what's the point of making friends? If you don't mind, I prefer to be on my own.' She gave him a pointed look and after a while he finally took the hint and stood up.

'Okay, have it your way, but if you get lonely, come find me.' He tried out his winning smile on her again, but she just glared at him until he retreated to the safety of his friends. She heard them whispering, but didn't care. She also heard a soft chuckle coming from her left, but she refused to look at *him* again.

The whole lot of them could go hang for all she cared.

Chapter Three

The geometry lesson was almost too easy and Rain solved the problems they were given in record time, then sat gazing out of the window. *Maybe I should have taken a more difficult class? At least then I wouldn't be bored and I could've annoyed everyone by not being able to complete the homework ...* But at least this way she didn't need to even try and think too much.

Her next class was Home Ed, which would apparently take up the rest of the morning, and she made her way to a different part of the school for that. It turned out to be in a big room divided into sections like miniature kitchens, which she had to admit was kind of cool. After introducing herself to the teacher, she went to sit at the one furthest away in a corner.

The rest of the class filed in. There were only eight other people and the teacher, Mrs Beech, clapped her hands and told them to divide into pairs. 'This is great. We have five kitchenettes, so we'll have five teams of two people. You and you, over there ...' Finally, there was only Rain left, but just as she thought she'd end up on her own, a latecomer sauntered into the room.

'Ah, Jesse, how nice of you to join us at last,' Mrs Beech said sarcastically. 'Get your butt over there and join the new girl, please.'

Of course it had to be him. Who else? Rain sighed. How annoying was that? He grinned at her in a way that made her heart flip over uncomfortably, but she didn't respond. Instead, she concentrated on the teacher's instructions while he sat down.

'Today we're going to cook *tortilla*, a mouth-wateringly delicious Spanish omelette.'

'Don't you mean Mexican?' someone asked. 'Like for *burritos*?'

'No, this is totally different. A round omelette with sliced potatoes inside,' Mrs Beech explained. 'Now here's what you have to do.' The teacher talked while she handed out the recipe and ingredients to everyone – potatoes, three eggs, an onion and a bottle of olive oil. 'Salt and pepper should be in your cupboards, and you know where the saucepans are. Get to it, teams. I'm going to be tasting your efforts, and whoever makes the best one gets a dessert I made earlier.'

Rain stood up and grabbed the bag of potatoes, which she held out to Jesse. 'You want to peel these while I cut the onion?' she asked without much enthusiasm.

'Uhm, right.' He took the bag somewhat reluctantly and poured the contents into the sink, then hunted around in a drawer for something to peel them with. He came up with a small but sharp knife, and Rain stared at him with raised eyebrows.

'You're going to peel them with that?'

'Sure, why not?'

'Hello? Because it's kind of easier to use a potato peeler? Or don't you have those in this country?' She picked through the drawer and found one. 'Here, try this. Works a treat, trust me.'

'Yeah, whatever.' He wasn't grinning any more, she noticed, which was good. He was obviously way too big for his boots and could do with taking down a peg or two.

She concentrated on peeling and chopping the onion, fast and efficiently. Then she found a large non-stick frying pan and filled it almost to the brim with olive oil before adding the onion. She had done a Cordon Bleu cookery course at Blakeborough, so making a little omelette wasn't going to tax her cooking skills. Besides, she adored tortilla and was quite looking forward to eating it. That would save her having to go to the cafeteria at all and also spare her from running into the likes of Cody Knight. *Excellent.*

She looked over to Jesse and couldn't stop an involuntary giggle from escaping, even though she had been determined to stay cool around him at all times. 'Uhm, I think we're meant to finish this today, not, like, next century,' she said. He had only peeled half a potato so far and seemed to be struggling with the peeler.

He glared at her. 'Okay, Miss Smart-Ass, if you're so fast, you do it. It's not like I want to know how anyway.'

Without a word, she took the potato and peeler from his hands and ignored the little shockwave that went through her arm at the small contact between them. No point thinking about that, she told herself. *Been there, done that, so not doing it again.* She continued where he'd left off. She had the potato finished in seconds. 'Ta-dah,' she said and handed it to him with a flourish. 'Can you manage to chop it into thin slices, do you think? Or would you like me to do that for you, sir?'

'Shut up, new girl,' he muttered, but he took the potato and began to chop it up. At least he seemed able to do that, thank the Lord. Rain picked up the next potato and started peeling again.

When Jesse was done chopping, Rain turned on the cooker and soon had the onion and potato slices simmering. Jesse seemed happy to just watch and handed her the salt and pepper without her having to ask for it, so she could add seasoning.

'So why are you here if you don't want to be?' he finally said, just when the silence between them was becoming a bit of a strain and the effort of not looking his way was starting to get to her. His lazy voice was pitched low, but no one else would have heard him in any case because the rest of the class was being incredibly noisy.

'Just got expelled from boarding school for sleeping in my boyfriend's bed,' she replied, keeping her voice down too and trying to sound as if it was the most natural thing in the world. 'And getting drunk on tequila.' She heard him draw in a hissing breath of surprise and stared up at him. 'Attending Northbrooke High for a while is my punishment, but I'm hoping to get out of it soon,' she added.

'Right.' He was looking at her as if he wasn't quite sure she was telling the truth.

'What, you don't believe me? Ask my parents. Or Dr A. It's true.'

'Yeah, okay, I believe you.' He changed the subject abruptly and nodded at the frying pan. 'I take it you know what to do next with that?'

Rain nodded. 'Yep. Watch and learn, Emo Boy.'

He laughed at that. 'I'm not emo. I'm in a band, but we're more like alternative rock or pop punk. None of that angst shit.'

'Whatever. You're dressed in black and you've dyed your hair. Seems pretty emo to me.' She should have known he'd be in a band. His type always were and she had to admit he looked the part with his torn black jeans, spiky hair and eyebrow piercing, not to mention those tattoos.

'No way. FYI this is my natural colour.' He pretended to fluff his hair, like stupid models did on TV when advertising hair products, and she almost giggled again.

She played along with the idea. 'Ah, not because you're worth it.'

'Exactly.'

She put her head to one side and looked at him more closely. 'Actually, you do look kind of like Rick Linden of *Snake*. If you know who that is.'

'Duh, doesn't everyone? He's like, one of the best guitarists ever.'

'Yes, well, he has black hair and blue eyes, doesn't he? Or maybe he dyed his.'

Jesse shrugged. 'No idea.'

She decided to concentrate on the tortilla. She didn't know why she was talking to him so much anyway, but she couldn't seem to help herself. 'Could you get me two plates, please?' He reached into a cupboard and handed them down. 'And some oven gloves, if there are any.'

The knack with making tortilla was the way you turned it, a Spanish neighbour of theirs had taught her a couple of summers earlier. You had to pour off most of the olive oil, mash the cooked potatoes firmly into the rest, add the eggs, fry for a while, then tip the omelette onto a plate. After that you put another plate on top and turned the two over before sliding the omelette back into the frying pan to fry the other side. That way it stayed in one piece. She performed this manoeuvre without any trouble with Jesse watching intently.

'Neat,' was his only comment.

Mrs Beech came over just as Rain slid the finished omelette back onto a plate. It was a perfect unbroken circle, lightly browned to just the right shade and giving off a heavenly smell. 'Looking good, new girl,' Mrs Beech said. 'I hope Jesse helped?' She gave him a sceptical look as if she was used to him being useless at cooking. It made Rain want to defend him for some reason.

'Yes, he peeled and chopped the potatoes and acted as my assistant chef,' she replied, without looking his way.

'Great, teamwork, that's what I like to see. Keep it up and I might even give you a D this term instead of flunking you, Devlin. Okay, let me taste this.' Mrs Beech took the fork Jesse held out to her and cut off a piece of tortilla. 'Mmm-hmm, perfect. Ten out of ten, good stuff.'

She swept off to try the other teams' efforts. Jesse smiled at Rain and held up his hand for a high five. 'Thanks.' She obliged, although she didn't really want to touch him. It sent shivers down her spine.

'Are we allowed to eat it now?' she asked. The cooking smells were making her stomach grumble.

'In a minute. Wait till the old dragon makes her choice in case she has to taste it again.'

Mrs Beech spoke up. 'Okay, class, decision-making time. Today, I'm going to give the dessert to ... Rain and Jesse. Here you are, great effort.'

She bustled over with two containers of what looked like home-made chocolate mousse. Rain was pleased despite herself. At least this class wasn't so bad, she could put up with this. And chocolate mousse was her favourite.

'Result!' Jesse muttered.

'Okay, dig in everybody, then do the washing up in record time, please.' Mrs Beech's voice was raised above the din that had erupted as everyone started talking again. 'No cheating. I'll be checking that everything's clean or you'll have to do it again.'

There were two bar stools at the end of the counter in each kitchenette and Rain and Jesse sat down to eat. 'She's right, this is damned good,' Jesse said after a couple of mouthfuls. 'Where'd you learn to cook?'

'At my school. We all had to do Cordon Bleu classes, in case we wanted to be chalet girls for a season or two.'

'Shallow what?'

'Not shallow, *chalet* girls. You know, in the ski resorts?' He looked blank, so she had to explain. 'In the Swiss mountains at the ski resorts, people come and stay for their holidays in little houses called chalets. And they're looked after by one or two girls, depending on the size of the house. These chalet girls have to do all the cooking and cleaning so that the skiers can just enjoy themselves. It's a popular way among my friends – er, my former friends – to spend part of your gap year.'

'Gap yah?'

'Yeeeear. Gap year, you know, like when you have a year off to work or bum around before going off to college?'

'Right. Sounds like hard work to me, that shallying thing.' Jesse made a face.

'Yes, it is, but at the same time you get a lot of time off for skiing all winter and you're there to catch the best of the snow whenever that is. What could be better?'

'I guess. Well, you sure can cook anyway. Let's try this chocolate thing.' He did and closed his eyes in an expression of pure bliss. 'Oh, yeah, baby. This is awesome.'

Rain had to agree and closed her own eyes to savour the heavenly mousse. When she opened them again, she was disconcerted to find Jesse reaching out to her mouth where he wiped a blob of chocolate off from the corner with one finger.

'You're being messy,' he grinned and then licked the surplus mousse off his finger with an exaggerated gesture. Rain felt her cheeks heat up again and cursed inwardly. 'You know, you blush an awful lot for someone who's been caught sleeping with your boyfriend,' he commented casually, the look in his eyes teasing again.

Rain glared at him. 'I just have very white skin,' she snapped, 'and it's hot in here.'

'Sure, sure.' He was still grinning and she wanted to hit him, but didn't. That would involve touching him, which was a definite no-no. 'Guess that's why you look like such an Ice Maiden, then,' he continued. 'All that pale skin and hair, huh?'

Rain didn't know how to answer that. She did have a very pale English rose type of complexion and thick, naturally blonde hair. If that made her look like an Ice Maiden, there wasn't much she could do about it other than go sunbathing, which wasn't an option here now autumn had set in.

'Since you did the cooking, I'll wash up,' he offered to her surprise and Rain just nodded and helped him carry the crockery over to the sink. He didn't seem to have any difficulty doing that at least, so she guessed he had to help out at home a lot. Unlike most of the boys she'd known at Blakeborough, who were used to Filipina maids doing things like that for them. She helped him by drying everything and putting the stuff back in the cupboards.

At the end of the lesson, he nodded at her and said, 'Look forward to eating some more of your cooking next week. Later, Ice Girl.'

Rain felt some of the anger inside her thaw a little and realised that she would look forward to it as well. Maybe her short stay here wouldn't be quite as bad as she'd feared after all.

When she came out into the corridor, however, she found him with his arm round a stunning little brunette, who was gazing up at him with a look that said she owned him. *Jeez, buy a leash why don't you*, Rain thought in disgust. She passed them and Jesse looked up as if he was going to say something, but Rain turned her head away and hurried off.

So he had a girlfriend. Big deal. Of course he would, a guy like that would never be single. And Rain didn't care.

She'd had it with boyfriends. *Seriously*.

Chapter Four

Jesse held onto Amber so she wouldn't turn her head and see where he was looking. Because the truth was, he couldn't take his eyes off the new girl and wanted to watch her for as long as he could.

She sauntered off, all tall and leggy, like a supermodel but with the right sort of curves. There was no doubt she was totally gorgeous to look at, despite her almost permanent scowl and stand-offish ways. That blonde hair would be great to run your hands through and her generous mouth was made for kissing. He'd been very tempted to do just that when he removed the chocolate mousse earlier, but that would probably have made her run off screaming. He grinned to himself as he thought back on their conversation. He'd managed to make her smile at least once though, so she wasn't completely immune to him, even though she tried to make out that she was.

Ice Maiden, he'd called her, and that was the vibe she gave off, but he was pretty sure that underneath the hard exterior, she was vulnerable. She looked like she'd been hurt, badly, and he had a terrible urge to reach out and pull her into his arms to comfort her. Sadly, he already had his arms full and Amber was nothing if not demanding.

'Hello? I'm talking to you.' She poked him in the chest.

'Huh?' He looked down at her, trying to remember what she'd just said.

'I said, are we going to have lunch now?' Amber's brown eyes, big and luminous like those of a beautiful deer, perfectly made up to lengthen the lashes and enhance the colour, were fixed on him and she was frowning at his lack of attention.

'Not me, I'm really full. I just had Home Ed, babe. But I'll sit with you while you eat if you want?'

'No, that's okay. I'm on a diet, so I think I'll skip lunch today.'

'You shouldn't do that, you know. You don't need to diet, honest.' He frowned at her, impatient at her constant striving for perfection in the looks department. She was fine the way she was and if she got any skinnier, she'd disappear since she wasn't very big to begin with. Most people compared her to a porcelain doll, perfectly proportioned, but in miniature. She brought out the protective instinct in all the guys because she looked so fragile, yet sexy at the same time. A great combination, but one that was starting to irritate him a little because he knew now that there was nothing fragile about her. She had a core of pure steel and was used to getting her way in all things.

'Let's go find somewhere to make out instead.' She smiled at him, the beguiling smile that had so attracted him when he first noticed her the year before, but for some reason he didn't find it quite as appealing today.

'Uhm, better not. I can't afford to get detention again if we're caught. My dad will skin me alive,' he lied. His dad couldn't care less about what he got up to at school, or anywhere else for that matter, but Amber didn't know that. She never asked much about him and that was fine by him.

Amber pouted prettily. 'Fine, well, let's go outside at least. It's so stuffy in here.'

'Okay, whatever you say.'

Jesse threw one last look over his shoulder and watched Rain disappear around a corner. Even if she hadn't been so tall, she would have stood out from the crowd. Her long hair shimmered in the sunlight from the windows as she swung it impatiently over one shoulder. He took in what she was wearing – black leggings, knee-high suede boots and a denim miniskirt so short it was almost indecent – and stared at the way her hips swayed when she walked. She could have been on a catwalk, her easy strides sexy and confident. It was no wonder several guys stopped to gawk after her, although she didn't seem to notice.

He closed his eyes for a moment and shook himself mentally. *What the hell is the matter with me?* This was crazy. It had to stop. He already had everything he wanted. Pulling Amber tight to his side, he walked off in the opposite direction.

Rain had to swallow the urge to laugh out loud when she saw the expression on Coach Rivers' face as she turned up for soccer practice after school that afternoon. His jaw fell and he couldn't seem to take his eyes off the large area of naked skin between the bottom of her T-shirt and the very low waistband of her tracksuit trousers. She'd had to ring her mother and ask her to bring these in, since she hadn't brought any gym clothes, together with her football boots. An unzipped hoodie completed her outfit.

'Dr A said to tell you I could try out for soccer,' she told the coach, who closed his mouth and nodded, still momentarily speechless. 'I'm Rain Mackenzie.'

'Rain. Right. Try-out.' Rain was beginning to wonder if the man was a parrot or a human, when he pulled himself together and added, 'Okay. You got cleats?' She lifted one foot and showed him the underside of her shoes. He nodded approval. 'Good.'

'So what do I do? Is there a test or something?' she asked curtly, ignoring the wolf whistles that were coming from somewhere out on the pitch. She was used to dealing with boys; there had been plenty of them at Blakeborough, most of them as idiotic as the ones here. *I'll soon show them.*

'Er, have you played before?'

'Yes.' *Would I want to play otherwise?* But she didn't say that out loud.

'So you know the rules of the game?'

'Yep. Including the offside rule,' Rain added before he could ask. *Honestly, why did so many men think women were incapable of grasping that simple concept?*

'Right,' the coach said again. 'We were going to start with some footwork drills. I guess the best thing is if you just join in and I'll, er, assess you.'

Coach Rivers shook his head as if he was clearing it of some kind of mental blockage, and turned to call his team to order. 'Okay, everyone, grab a ball each and start with basic triangles and juggling please. I want to see some fast footwork here, people!'

Rain took a ball from the net someone was holding out and ran out onto the field to find herself a clear space. She'd noticed Jesse was on the team as soon as she'd arrived, but he'd kept away from her and thankfully hadn't been one of the guys whistling at her. Now she made sure to put some distance between them and concentrated on the ball. She knew what the coach was asking for, since she'd had to do this kind of training at Blakeborough, although she looked to make sure she was doing the same thing as everyone else.

After a while, Coach Rivers shouted for someone to put some cones out. 'Come on, cone drills everyone, line up!'

Lines of flattish sports cones were laid along the pitch with narrow gaps in between. Everyone lined up and took turns to dribble the ball with the outside of their foot in a zig-zag pattern, weaving through the cones. Rain managed most of them and only missed a couple of times, but then not many of the other team members were perfect either.

The coach had them do some other exercises to improve their command of the ball and Rain quite enjoyed these. Speed and ball control were required, and a lot of jumping from foot to foot, so it was a great work-out while being fun at the same time.

'Everyone over here, please,' the coach called out. 'Split into pairs and practise defence against another player. Scissor moves, hesitation moves, feints, whatever you can get away with. Just make sure you fool the other guy.'

Rain waited to see who her partner would be. She didn't know anyone, so didn't really care. To her annoyance, however, a familiar voice sounded from behind her. 'I'll do Rain.' She swivelled round and came face to face with Jesse, while the rest of the team started laughing at the double meaning of his words.

'You wish. Are you following me around or something?'

'Of course, Ice Girl. It's my mission in life, don't you know?' He smiled at her in that aggravating way that made her have to take a deep breath, then he nodded towards the field. 'Come on, let's go. I want to see what you can do.'

'I bet you do,' she muttered and followed him onto the field. Out of the corner of her eye she noticed that his girlfriend was busy with cheerleading practice nearby, but he didn't seem to be paying her any attention. 'Are you sure you're allowed to play with me?' she asked.

'What do you mean?' He stopped and looked at her with questioning eyes.

She nodded in his girlfriend's direction. 'You're being watched.'

He frowned slightly, then shrugged. 'We're just playing ball. It's not like I'm going to throw you down onto the grass and ravish you or something. Although come to think of it …' He laughed suddenly and pretended to rush at her.

She sidestepped neatly. 'Get lost,' she said, but in a good-natured way. Somehow she didn't mind this verbal sparring with him. It made the knot of anger inside her dissolve a bit.

'Right, now come over here, this is where you stand,' he instructed, pointing at a spot on the ground. 'I'm going to dribble around you and you have to stop me.'

'Duh! I may be blonde but I'm not completely thick, you know.'

'Okay, okay, I'm just trying to be nice. You won't catch the opposing team giving you a break just because you're a girl.'

Rain sent him a glare. 'I have played soccer before, actually. It's one of our two national sports, in case you didn't know. "The beautiful game", we call it, and it's not like American football where you have to wear tons of protection just to avoid being killed.'

'Hey, that's one of *our* national games you're talking about,' he protested, but he was smiling so Rain knew he was just teasing again.

'Oh, never mind, just dribble the damn ball, will you.'

He did and although it took her a while because his footwork was so fast, she eventually managed to stop him quite a few times. The first time she did it, Jesse looked at her, his blue eyes opening wide. 'Damn, Ice Girl, I'm impressed. But maybe that was just beginner's luck?'

'No way. Try again.' Rain concentrated even harder and proved to him that her skills owed nothing to luck whatsoever. She was just very good at ball games, always had been, although the fact that he was deliberately bumping into her to throw her off balance was very distracting, and he slipped past her more often than she would have liked. Having him so close played havoc with her senses and she found it really difficult to keep her eyes on the ball instead of on him.

Coach Rivers came over to watch them and he was impressed too. 'Wow, girl, that's not bad you know,' he said, which sounded like it might be praise indeed. Rain just nodded. She didn't really care what he thought, but it was kind of nice to be taken seriously.

'I can't guarantee you'll get to play, but I'm happy to have you on the team as a possible substitute, if that's okay with you?'

'Yeah, why not?' Rain hadn't expected to be centre forward or anything. At least she was fulfilling the criteria of doing an extracurricular activity. Whether she actually got to play or not didn't matter.

Jesse suggested they swap places after a while and smiled to himself since this gave him the opportunity to watch Rain instead of the ball. He did everything he could to stop her from dribbling the ball around him, including blocking her path with his body. A thrill raced through him every time his shoulder came into contact with hers, or he caught the scent of her hair as it flicked past him. She wasn't bad at soccer. It was clear she really had played before and although he doubted she'd get to play any games, she seemed to know what she was doing.

Out of the corner of his eye, he could see Amber frowning in his direction, but he pretended not to notice. He'd tell her later that the coach hadn't given him a choice, he'd had to partner Rain.

'What the hell did you just do?' Rain asked, sounding exasperated as he blocked her for the third time by flicking the ball away from her with a deft move.

'Like this,' he said, moving to stand next to her to show her what he'd done in slow motion. 'You've got to make your opponent believe they're going to get away with it, then fool them at the last minute.'

'Okay, I get it.' She stepped away from him, blushing again, and he suppressed another smile. She probably wouldn't appreciate him mentioning her tendency to pink cheeks again – once a day was enough, he figured. It was interesting that she seemed to blush so much around him though. Perhaps it was a good sign?

He gave himself a talking to. He already had a girlfriend and Rain had said she wasn't staying long, so there was no point making a move on her. *Give it a rest,* he told his conscience, *I'm just having a bit of fun, no big deal.* 'Okay, then, do your worst,' he said to Rain and smiled at her.

It took her a few tries before she got the hang of it, and although she'd never make a brilliant forward, she didn't do too badly. She seemed dissatisfied with herself, however, and she looked a bit annoyed when the coach called out for them to stop.

'That was crap,' she said.

'No, it wasn't. Some of those moves can be hard at first. It's just practice, so give yourself a break. When did you start playing?'

'A couple of years ago.'

'Well, there you go. Most of us have been kicking a ball around since we were knee-high, so you're fairly new to this. You did good.'

Coach Rivers shouted out orders again. 'I want everyone to jog around the edge of the pitch five times, then we're going to do some sprinting. We have to practise hard so we don't mess up any chances of winning our next game.'

There were groans from some members of the team while they all set off around the field, but Jesse noticed that Rain stayed silent. She began to run with easy strides, making it look effortless, and he fell into step beside her.

'Do you jog a lot?' he asked, curious to know more about her.

'Yes, a couple of times a week,' she said. 'I like being outdoors. Gyms are so smelly and usually way too hot. Plus everyone's watching everyone else in the mirrors, posing, you know? So pretentious.'

He smiled. 'For sure.' So that was how she kept herself in such good shape, he thought. He couldn't help comparing that with Amber's endless dieting and silly step classes and whatever. Jogging was so much more natural, and he hadn't noticed Rain stinting herself on the food in Home Ed either. She'd tucked in to her half of the tortilla and finished every last blob of chocolate mousse. Yet, there wasn't an ounce of fat on her except where there ought to be. He took a deep breath and steered his thoughts away from thinking about that.

Jesse liked running and without thinking, he started humming under his breath, using the pounding of their feet as rhythm in his head.

'You forget your iPod or something?' Rain asked as they turned a corner of the field.

'Huh? Oh, no, I was just trying out a song. You know, composing in my head.'

'I see. Do you do that a lot?'

'Sure, all the time. I told you, I'm in a band.'

She nodded. 'Cool. Must be fun.'

He shrugged. 'Yeah, I like it.'

They ran along in silence for a while after that, but then he couldn't help asking, 'So why are you doing soccer?'

'Why not? Seemed like a good idea at the time.'

'We have a game on Saturday, two hours away by coach. Did they tell you that?'

'No.' She sighed. 'Even more time wasted.'

'What do you mean?'

'I was hoping to spend as little time as possible at this school,' she explained. 'I hadn't reckoned on doing extra stuff. Do we all have to go on that trip, then?'

'Yup, afraid so. Crack of dawn outside school on Saturday morning. Seven a.m. Sucks.'

'Great,' she groaned.

They jogged along in silence after that and whenever they passed the part of the field where Amber and her fellow cheerleaders were practising, Jesse made sure he wasn't too close to Rain. Amber was extremely jealous, despite the fact that she was sure she was the prettiest girl in school. Jesse figured it wouldn't be a good idea to give her any reason to dislike Rain. She could make Rain's life very difficult. Not that she looked like she'd care, but still.

Jesse and Rain were among the first to complete the five laps and Coach Rivers started them off on short sprints. Jesse was one of the fastest guys in the school and easily beat the others every time, but Rain was quick for a girl and managed to outrun some of the smaller guys.

'Not bad, you're pretty fast,' he commented to her after the third time and she smiled at last.

'It's my long legs. I suppose they have to be good for something.'

He looked her up and down, trying not to stare at her stunning midriff yet again. 'You don't like them?' How could she not? he wondered. They seemed perfect to him.

She shook her head. 'Most of the time it's not much fun being a giraffe girl and getting called names, but I'm used to it now.'

He smiled. 'I wouldn't call you that. More like supermodel material. I bet you could wear a sack and look good in it.'

She blinked in surprise and he swore inwardly. He hadn't meant to compliment her, the words had just slipped out.

'Er ... thank you. I think.'

'You're welcome. Race you one more time?'

'You're on.'

Jesse smiled broadly and thought to himself that soccer practice was going to be a hell of a lot more interesting from now on.

Chapter Five

'So how was your first day, darling?'

Sir Anthony was looking at his daughter across the dinner table and Rain made a face at him. 'Do you really want to know?'

He nodded and smiled, which almost made her smile back, although she resisted. She wasn't giving in that easily and she had to make sure he knew that she was still annoyed about having to stay here and attend Northbrooke High. Did he have any idea what he had condemned her to? Knowing him, he probably did, but that didn't excuse him one little bit.

'It was absolutely wonderful. I loved every minute and everyone was sooo sweet,' she trilled in a cheerful voice that sounded just as fake and sarcastic as she'd intended.

'Rain,' Sir Anthony warned, frowning now. 'Stop that.'

Rain and her father had always had a special bond and she knew that he didn't want her to be unhappy, really. She was usually able to twist him round her little finger. That was why she'd counted on being back in England fairly soon and still did. She sighed.

'Okay, then. I survived all my classes, I was ace in Home Ed and I had soccer practice. It was all a dead bore, just as I'd expected. And the people,' she rolled her eyes. 'They have to be seen to be believed. Like something out of an American soap opera. Cheerleaders with silly pom-poms, for heaven's sake. I really don't know how any sane person would make it through a whole year here.'

Sir Anthony's eyebrows rose a fraction. 'Soccer practice?' he said, ignoring the rest of what she'd told him. 'I didn't realise they had a girls' team here.'

'They don't. I had to train with the boys.' Rain shrugged. 'The Seniors have to do some kind of activity after school, so that's what I chose. You know, I might have made captain at Blakeborough. Here I'll be lucky if I get to play at all.'

'Guess you shouldn't have got yourself expelled, then.' Sir Anthony said mildly.

'Oh, Dad.' Rain made a face. 'Come on, you know I should be back in England. I'd be able to play on a girls' team there.' She was hoping he'd take the hint, but he didn't comment. 'Maybe I should try American football instead?' she muttered. 'Then when I break every bone in my body, at least I won't have to go to school for a while.'

It was Sir Anthony's turn to sigh and her mother sent her a look of exasperation. 'Really, Rain, do stop being so melodramatic.'

'That's easy for you to say. You don't have to go to Northbrooke High.'

'You wouldn't have had to either, if you'd behaved properly, like a well-brought-up young lady.'

Rain rolled her eyes. 'I *told* you, it wasn't my fault. At least, not all of it. We were just having a bit of fun.'

'You knew the rules and you broke them. Now you're suffering the consequences. That's the way of things.'

'Yes, while the others got off almost scot-free. Is that fair? Milo only got suspended for two weeks and—'

Her mother interrupted her. 'Because the midnight drinking feast was your idea. Let me tell you, it's not *fun* for your parents, who have to be ashamed of your behaviour.'

'Come, come, we've been over this already and what's done is done.' Sir Anthony tried to smooth things out as usual. He was always the mediator between Rain and her mother, who never seemed able to agree on anything. Rain didn't think she'd ever be the perfect daughter her mother wanted. As for ladylike behaviour? *Not a chance!* That was just boring.

She sometimes wished she was more like her brother or sister. Rob, who was two years older than Rain, was in his second year of uni studying medicine in Edinburgh. Although he'd been a bit wild at school too, he was also seriously clever so he always got perfect grades, which seemed to make up for any other faults as far as her parents were concerned. Their younger sister Raven, who was still at Blakeborough, was also a brainiac, and much less trouble than Rain, or so it seemed. *If only I could be more like her.* But she wasn't.

Changing the subject back to the original one, Sir Anthony asked, 'And did you enjoy it? The soccer, I mean?'

She considered telling him she'd hated it, but he would know she was lying, so she told the truth. 'Yes, it was okay. It's kind of harder having to compete with guys though. I just couldn't get the hang of some of those stupid defence moves. Not that it matters. I don't suppose they'll let me play in any games anyway.'

'No, probably not. Any other girls on the team?'

Rain could see the teasing glint in her father's eyes. 'No, just me.'

'Hmm, bet you made the other players' day, then,' he laughed. 'What did the coach say?'

'He seemed a bit uncomfortable, but that's his problem, not mine. Actually, there were a few comments, but I ignored them. So childish.' She pulled a face again. 'The worst thing is I have to go with them to the next game, early on Saturday. Can someone give me a lift to the school, please? We're leaving at seven sharp, apparently. Or maybe I should call in sick? You don't really want to get up that early, do you?'

Sir Anthony smirked. 'No, don't worry, we'll get you there. Wouldn't want you to feel left out.'

'Ha, ha, very funny.'

'I'm serious,' he protested with another smile. 'You'll have fun, cheering on your team even if you don't get to participate.'

Rain got up and turned her back on her unfeeling father. 'Can't wait,' she muttered.

'What in tarnation is that smell, boy?' Tom Devlin came into the kitchen, sniffing the air with his nose wrinkled. 'You burned your dinner?'

Jesse turned towards his father and frowned. 'No, I'm cooking Spanish tortilla. Just learned how at school today, so I thought I'd try it out at home. Make a change from TV dinners.'

Tom peered into the frying pan with an expression of disgust. 'I don't like eggs,' he said.

'Since when? And this isn't just eggs. It's got potatoes and onions in it too, and we can have salad with it. I bought some. Mrs Beech said ...'

'Salad!' Tom cut in, outraged. 'I ain't eatin' no leaves and stuff. That's for cows and them skinny women on TV.'

'Dad ...'

'Get me a TV dinner, boy, and stop arguing with me. You eat that crap if you want to, but I'd like some real food if you don't mind. Got to keep my strength up.'

Jesse clamped his teeth together, more annoyed than he'd ever let on to his old man. *What's the matter with the guy?* He should be grateful that someone was cooking for him at all. 'Fine, whatever,' he said.

Tom pointed a finger at him warningly. 'And don't you take that tone with me, or I'll have to teach you another lesson.'

Jesse turned away, but almost swivelled around again when his father chuckled and said, 'Not turning pansy on me, are you? Cooking is for girls, or at least it was last time I heard.'

'Yeah, well, I don't see any girls around here,' Jesse said through gritted teeth, 'so if I want something decent to eat I have to make it myself. Doesn't make me gay.'

'If you say so.' The laughter was still in Tom's voice, however, and it made Jesse want to hit him. But he'd had enough violence from his father to last him a lifetime already, so he just clenched his fist tightly on the cooking implements and concentrated on turning the tortilla the way Rain had showed him. It worked perfectly and he was really pleased with the result. He determined to pay more attention in Home Ed in future, then he at least could eat some decent food.

While the tortilla cooked on the other side, he stuck a TV dinner in the microwave and handed it to his dad when the pinger went. Acting on autopilot, he grabbed a beer from the fridge, which he opened and put next to his father as well. He didn't expect or receive any thanks, just loaded his own plate with the delicious-smelling omelette and headed for his room.

He couldn't stand to even eat next to his dad. He hated his guts.

It had been this way for years now. Ever since his mother died when Jesse was ten. Up until that point his life had been bearable, but after that there was nothing good about it at all.

Why did you have to leave me with that miserable bastard, Mom? he wondered. *Why couldn't he have died instead?* Thinking that way made him feel guilty though, so he stared at his plate and tried to push everything else out of his mind. He looked around the room and realised there was nothing here he would miss. Nothing at all.

As soon as he turned eighteen he was leaving and never coming back.

'Hey, gorgeous. You in a better mood today?'

Rain sighed and looked up from putting stuff in her locker to find Cody leaning nonchalantly next to it, smiling at her. He was immaculately dressed in a Ralph Lauren shirt, logo clearly visible, and matching chinos. His hair looked like he'd blow-dried it for hours again to achieve the perfect style. She raised her eyebrows at him. Was he for real? An ego that size shouldn't be able to fit into a school this small, she thought.

'There was nothing wrong with my mood yesterday,' she replied. 'The problem was in the people who surrounded me.'

'Aw, you don't really mean that. I know, you're just playing hard to get. Is that how you do things in your country? 'Cause I can tell you, guys over here are more persistent. We know what we want and we go get it.'

'I'm sure you do,' Rain said drily. *But you're not getting me.*

'So is that a yes, then?'

'Yes to what?'

'You'll let me take you around today? Sit with us in the cafeteria? We'll have a ball, I swear.' He nodded in the direction of a group of his friends, who stood nearby watching the exchange. 'Everyone's dying to meet you. And they'll love that cute little accent of yours.'

'No. Thank you. And I don't have an accent. You do.' Rain tried to keep from gritting her teeth. *Jeez, this guy is thicker than five planks.* How could she get him to take no for an answer?

'What?' Cody laughed. 'Okay, I get you. You want to play Miss Unavailable for just a bit longer. Sure, sure, go right ahead, but I'm not giving up. Later.'

He flashed his white teeth at her again and she rolled her eyes. 'Wanker,' she muttered into her locker and continued with the task of unloading her stuff.

'That guy bothering you?'

Rain took a deep breath and straightened up again. 'Yes, but I took care of it.'

Jesse Devlin was now leaning his tattooed arm along the top of her open locker door. It was so close, Rain could see every detail of the intricate dragon that snaked up towards his broad shoulder. 'Cool,' he said. 'Just checking. Cody's an asshole so it would be my pleasure to beat him up for you. I'll take any excuse.'

'Thanks, but I can do that myself. He's so vain I'll just distract him with a mirror, then I can floor him easily.'

Jesse chuckled. 'I'd like to see that.'

'Stick around and you probably will very soon.' She glanced at his arm again. 'That must have taken ages. Wasn't it painful? And cost a small fortune?'

'What? Oh, that. Nah, not really. I know a guy at a tattoo parlour and he wanted someone to practise on. He got me drunk and set to work. Luckily he wasn't drunk himself, so it turned out okay. You like it?'

Rain surprised herself by saying, 'Yes, I wouldn't mind one myself.' She realised it was the truth, although previously she'd always thought tattoos a bit common. Annabelle had a dolphin on her ankle, and it had irritated Rain like mad, but Jesse's tattoos were different. More authentic somehow.

'I'll have to take you to see Steve. I bet he'd love to draw on you.' Jesse let his eyes travel down the length of her in a very suggestive way and Rain felt her cheeks flame. 'Be a shame to spoil that white skin though. It's kind of nice the way it is.'

Rain frowned at him to discourage this line of thought. 'Whatever. My mother would have a fit anyway, so it's out of the question. Maybe when I turn eighteen.'

'And when's that?'

'Not till next year, unfortunately. I'll only be seventeen in November, if you must know.'

'How come? I mean, why are you a Senior if you're only sixteen?'

'We start school a year earlier than you in the UK, usually when we've turned five, and because I was a precocious little brat they even let me begin a couple months early.'

Jesse smiled at that. 'I see. So what date's your birthday?'

'The twenty-fourth. Why?'

'Seriously? That's my birthday too, but I'll be eighteen.'

Rain blinked at him. 'You're kidding. You have the same birthday as me?'

'Yep, sure do.'

'Hmm. Well, if I'm still here then, we'll have to have a joint party.'

'Yeah, right.' He snorted. 'I don't do birthday parties. Haven't had one since I was, like, three or something.' He stared into the distance, his expression a bit sad, although he soon hid the pain in his eyes. Rain had a sudden urge to stroke his cheek and make him smile again.

'Really? Why?' she found herself asking.

He shrugged. 'Don't know. No money for stuff like that.' He straightened up suddenly and stopped lounging on her locker. 'Gotta go. Let me know if you need help braining that jerk Cody. Later.'

'Okay, thanks.'

Rain stared after him and wondered what was going through his mind. She had obviously hit a raw nerve about the birthday party thing, but she didn't know why. Surely, even if his parents were poor, they could have done some sort of party for him when he was little? But perhaps not.

It's none of my business and I don't care anyway. But she knew that she did and that worried her.

Jesse was tucking into his home-made sandwiches at lunchtime, glancing from time to time at Amber. She was sitting by his side picking at a chicken salad without actually eating much of it. He was becoming seriously worried about her and was just about to say so, when she looked over towards the door and stifled a giggle.

'What?' he said, following her gaze with his eyes. Rain had just walked into the cafeteria and was making her way over to the food counter, looking neither right nor left. Her strides were confident, as if she couldn't care less whether anyone was staring at her or not, even though she had to know that everyone was. She was the only newcomer after all, and nothing much exciting ever happened at Northbrooke High.

'What a dork,' Amber commented. 'Looks like a giraffe in drag.'

'Since when is it a crime to be tall? I'm tall.' Jesse frowned at her, remembering what Rain had told him the day before. It pissed him off that she'd been right about people calling her names.

'It isn't when you're a guy.' Amber stroked his arm and smiled at him to let him know just how much she appreciated his height. 'But for a girl, it's different.' She continued to stare at Rain, who had now joined the line. 'And what's with the outfit? She looks like Puss in Boots.'

Jesse took in what Rain was wearing today. The tightest white drainpipe jeans he'd ever seen, with a pair of high-heeled black boots over the top that reached halfway up her thighs like she was a Musketeer or something. This was combined with a long-sleeved white T-shirt and some sort of fake fur sleeveless jacket. Okay, so it was different to what other girls were wearing, but it looked good on Rain. Especially those tight jeans which hugged her perfect backside. Amber and her friends burst into renewed giggles and it made Jesse want to tell them to shut up. They were so immature at times.

He was sitting at a table with Amber, her gang of close

girlfriends and some of the jock boys they hung out with, including Cody Knight. Jesse could have been a jock himself, since he was good at most sports, but he hated the way they dressed and didn't have anything else much in common with them either. He only sat with them because of Amber and because it gave him a feeling of satisfaction to know that he'd won the prize they all wanted – her. He knew they couldn't understand what she saw in him and that pleased him even more.

'That's not what I would call her,' Cody said now, setting off a wave of suggestive nods and noises around the table. 'I'll take her any day. Here kitty, kitty, kitty …'

'Stop being such an asshole, Cody,' Jesse snapped. 'Besides, didn't I hear her tell you to get lost this morning?'

'Shut up, Devlin. She's just playing hard to get. Everyone knows English girls are easy. It won't be long till she's eating out of my hand.'

'Or somewhere lower,' someone added, sparking a new round of laughter.

'Yeah. Did you hear that she got kicked out of her old school for sleeping with some guy? She was caught by the principal – how sad is that?'

'She was not,' Jesse said. He didn't know why he was protesting her innocence when she'd told him herself that she'd been caught in her boyfriend's bed, but he couldn't stand to hear her being discussed like that by the stupid jocks. *Like they know anything about it.*

'And how the hell do you know?' Cody glared at him.

'She told me. In Home Ed. Mrs Beech made me sit next to her.'

'You didn't tell me that.' Amber pouted at him.

He shrugged. 'Wasn't important.'

'So give us the details,' Cody urged. 'What did she say?'

'Why should I tell you? It was a private conversation.

All you need to know is you're wrong,' Jesse said firmly. He gritted his teeth to stop himself from getting up and punching the guy. He really hoped Rain would make good on her promise and do it herself.

'Huh, you're just making that up. Besides,' Cody continued, smirking at Jesse, 'it's none of your business, is it? You've got your hands full already, literally.' He laughed again and eyed Amber's top, which was nicely filled out.

'Cody,' she squeaked in protest and glared at him, before putting a restraining hand on Jesse's arm as he'd half stood up, snarling at Cody. 'Forget it, Jesse, he's just kidding. And he's right anyway, what's it to you?'

'Nothing,' Jesse muttered, trying to calm down. Amber shot him a look through narrowed eyes and he stared back, eyes wide open. 'What? I was just defending a fellow tall person, okay? I had enough jokes about it when I was little.'

Amber's gaze softened and she leaned against him. 'Aw, we weren't picking on you, sweetie. You're just right, you know that.'

'Mm-hmm.' He had his mouth full of sandwich again, which was a good excuse not to answer. Amber pushed her salad away and started whispering something to her best friend, Becky. Jesse nudged her. 'Aren't you going to eat that?' He pointed at her food.

'No, you have it if you want. I'm not hungry.'

Jesse sighed, but helped himself to the chicken salad anyway. There was no point wasting good food and if she wanted to starve herself to death, maybe that was her problem. He didn't want to know.

Chapter Six

On Saturday morning Rain boarded the bus with only seconds to spare.

'Hey, girl, didn't think you were going to make it.' Coach Rivers was standing by the door, tapping one foot impatiently.

'Yes, well, I don't do mornings,' she muttered. Once on board, she found two empty seats and grabbed both. She didn't feel like talking to anyone, so she feigned sleep, spending the whole journey with her eyes closed. She sincerely hoped they didn't have many more away games before the season was over.

Like everyone else, she was already wearing the team uniform she'd been given the day before: football shorts, knee-high socks with shin guards inside and a long-sleeved T-shirt with a baggier short-sleeved overshirt in the school's colours of turquoise and white. She'd bought herself a matching tracksuit from the school shop, and she was glad she was wearing it over the uniform since it was a cold and rainy morning. The hoodie kept her warm. Everything fit fairly well and for once she was glad she was tall. She didn't feel out of place as she walked onto the pitch with the others, but she heard a few indrawn breaths from the other team as they caught sight of her.

'What's this, Rivers?' The rival coach came up to greet them and eyed Rain with a frown. 'Females on the team?'

Coach Rivers cleared his throat, looking embarrassed, but held his ground. 'Nothing in the rules that says they can't play,' he grunted. 'We've got to move with the times, you know.'

'Yeah, right.' The other coach snorted, but didn't make any further comments. 'Well, let's get started.'

As she'd expected, Rain sat on a bench for the first hour. She'd been prepared not to care about her team, but to her surprise she was totally into the game from the word go and shouted encouragement same as the other substitutes. When one of her teammates scored a goal after a pass from Jesse, she jumped up with everyone else and allowed the guy next to her to high-five her without thinking about it. She almost began to feel a part of things. Perhaps this was what her father had meant, she thought, and he'd been right.

'Go, Coyotes!' she chanted with the others, having been told that was the name of the school team.

At half-time, the Northbrooke team led by one goal to nil, but then everything started to go wrong. First, the other team equalised. Then one of the Northbrooke guys hurt himself when he collided with one of the rival team members and had to be substituted, and another one was hit so hard on the nose by a ball that he fainted. The field was thick with mud by this time, as the rain had continued to fall steadily throughout the morning, and one of their best players slipped and twisted his ankle.

'Damn it all,' Coach Rivers shouted, banging his fist onto the bench next to him. He looked at the remaining substitutes and his gaze settled on Rain. 'Okay,' he sighed. 'Out you go, girl. Show 'em what you can do.'

'Me?' Rain squeaked. 'But what about …?' She looked around at the others, who she was sure would be a lot better than her. Not that she'd ever seen them play.

'No, I want you. Come on, hurry, do some warm-ups. We haven't got all day. Go, girl. I know you can do it. I saw what you did in practice.'

'Well, if you're sure?' She removed the tracksuit and did some stretches and jumps to get her blood circulating and her muscles warmed up, then she made sure her French plait wasn't in the way and marched onto the field. Some of the guys on the other team smirked when they saw her coming. It made Rain mad as hell, so she narrowed her eyes at everyone she passed and gave them a dirty look. She heard chuckles behind her but ignored them and concentrated on what needed to be done. The coach had assigned her to the right forward position and she was determined not to let him down.

The referee blew his whistle and the game got under way again. She knew their opponents would think her easy to deal with, so Rain pretended to look a bit girly and helpless at first. Jesse, who was in the centre now, threw her a questioning glance, and she winked at him, which made his mouth quirk up as he cottoned on. She ran back and forth with her teammates, but didn't do much to participate, hoping to lull their opponents into a false sense of security. When they started to more or less ignore her, she looked over at Jesse and nodded slightly. He made as if to pass the ball to another teammate, then spun round and sent it flying towards Rain instead.

She caught it and controlled it with her right foot, then set off up the pitch towards the goalkeeper. Jesse was with her – she could see him out of the corner of her eye – and the guys behind her helped clear the way by blocking or intercepting opponents if they came anywhere near her. Rain kept running, dribbling the ball and heading for the right hand corner of the goal. When she got close, she saw the goalie watching her, getting ready to intercept what he probably thought would be a feeble girly attempt at scoring. She sent him a dazzling smile and pretended to hesitate, while fluttering her eyelashes a few times as if she was getting flustered and nervous. She tried her best to look feminine and helpless.

The ruse seemed to work since his eyes widened and he grinned at her. His expression was slightly patronising like he felt sorry for her. When Rain was sure he was watching her face, rather than her feet, she suddenly passed the ball to her left, where she knew Jesse would be. He took his chance and slammed it into the goal with a hefty kick, taking the goalie by complete surprise.

'Hey!' the guy shouted in protest, as if it wasn't his fault they'd scored, but the Northbrooke team had erupted into cheers and yells, so he was soon drowned out. Rain sent him another smile, then ran over to congratulate Jesse.

'Go Jesse! You rock!' their teammates shouted and thumped them both on the back, jumping up and down in a big group hug. Rain felt adrenaline rushing through her and realised she was really enjoying this. She tried to tell herself it was no big deal, but the truth was it was exhilarating.

'Way to go, Rain.' Jesse grinned at her. 'They'll have a hard time beating us now.'

'All thanks to you,' she commented, smiling back.

'Nah, you set it up. Good work, partner. Must be my excellent coaching.'

'Don't flatter yourself.'

He bent to whisper in her ear. 'Although I saw what you did to that poor goalie – not really fair play. Most players don't use their eyelashes in the game.'

She pretended innocence and opened her eyes wide. 'What? Can't a girl smile at the opposition? I was just being friendly.'

'That depends on how you do it,' he chuckled. 'Bet he's really pissed off with himself now, falling for that kind of trick.'

'I don't know what you mean,' she replied, but she couldn't stop herself from laughing. It wasn't her problem if the other team's goalkeeper was a schmuck. She was just glad to have shown everyone that she wasn't a burden to the team, even if she had cheated a little. No one else seemed to have noticed.

Her euphoria lasted until it was time to shower and change. She was stopped by Coach Rivers on her way to the girls' locker room.

'Sorry, Rain, but the school janitor doesn't seem to have opened up the girls' section today. I guess he figured we'd only bring a team of boys. It's ... er, the norm after all. So you'll have to change in the ladies' bathroom and shower when you get home.'

'What? You're kidding, right?' Rain stared at him in disbelief. She was tired and extremely muddy and she wanted a shower. Now. 'Come on, I look like I've been mud wrestling!'

The coach seemed to consider the subject closed, because he walked into the boy's changing room without another word, leaving Rain to seethe quietly.

'No way. I'm not going back on the bus like this,' she muttered. 'Two hours being uncomfortable and smelly? I don't think so. I'm having a shower whether you like it or not, mister.'

With determined steps Rain followed him in, ignoring the cries of outrage that greeted her. The team had only just got inside, so no one was in a state of complete undress yet, which was a relief. She didn't know why they were making such a fuss anyway. Honestly, it wasn't as if she'd never seen a naked guy before. They weren't living in the Middle Ages.

'Hey, what's she doing in here, Coach? That's not allowed.'

'Miss Mackenzie, what do you think you're doing? This is just not acceptable.' Coach Rivers looked as scandalised as most of the others, although Rain now caught a few smirks and grins from some of her teammates. Some even started to encourage her to take her own clothes off, humming a well-known striptease song. She ignored them.

'I have a right to a shower, same as everyone else,' Rain said, trying to sound confident even though she was quaking inside now. *Maybe this wasn't such a good idea after all?*

'Impossible. You've got to get out of here right away or —'

Rain cut him off. She couldn't give in now. 'Aw, come on, Coach. Don't be so sexist. All you have to do is stand guard. I won't be long, I promise.'

'Well, I ...' Coach Rivers was clearly floundering, obviously not used to dealing with headstrong females.

Rain looked around and fixed her gaze on Jesse, because he was one of the few who hadn't protested at her presence. Thankfully, he had only got as far as taking off his shirt. She tried not to stare at his chest, which was well muscled, as was his washboard stomach. No tattoos there, so it was all on full view, making her wish she'd kept her eyes on the floor.

She took a deep breath and waited while the coach opened and closed his mouth a few times, clearly undecided. 'I don't know. I guess you have a right, since you're part of the team, but ...'

Jesse stepped forward and said calmly, 'I seem to remember there's a shower cubicle in the corner with a door. I'll stand guard, coach. Come on, Rain.'

Loud whistles and catcalls, together with a few lewd suggestions, greeted his words, but she pretended not to hear them and Jesse motioned for her to follow him. As soon as they were out of sight she breathed a sigh of relief.

'Over here.' The cubicle he indicated had a fairly sturdy door, although when she looked closer it didn't have a locking mechanism and there was a gap at both top and bottom. As if he had read her thoughts, however, Jesse said, 'I'll be right outside, and I won't let anyone past. Go on, get in there.' She didn't need to be told twice and for some reason she trusted him.

'Okay, thanks.'

She only glanced over the top once and saw nothing but Jesse's solid back. He was apparently as good as his word, so she undressed quickly and showered as fast as she could, washing her long hair at record speed. She finished and wrapped a towel round herself.

'Jesse? Could you hand me my bag, please?'

'Sure.' His voice sounded a bit husky, but the bag she'd left outside quickly appeared over the top of the cubicle. When she was dressed again, she came out and Jesse turned around. 'Your turn,' she said. 'Thanks, Jesse, I appreciate it.'

'No problem.'

'I'm, er ... going to wait outside.'

'That might be a good idea.' She couldn't read his expression, which seemed to be carefully neutral, but that was probably just as well, she thought. Relieved to have this over and done with, she fled, followed by more catcalls and whistles from the other cubicles. Along the way she saw a few sights she probably shouldn't have, but for once she didn't blush and she was proud of herself for making it into the fresh air with her head held high.

Thank God for Jesse. Without him she'd never have pulled it off.

Jesse stared after her until she disappeared out of sight, then went into the closed shower cubicle himself and leaned on the wall. The cool tiles against his back calmed down his racing heartbeat, but his breathing refused to go back to normal.

Damn her, why does she have to be so gorgeous?

Although he'd only peeked once, quickly, before everyone else came into the shower room, he knew the image of Rain covered in soap and water would stay with him for a long time, even though she'd had her back to him. She had the most perfect behind he'd ever seen, and with all that wet hair hanging down, she'd been a truly beautiful sight. He clenched his fists, trying to forget.

He shouldn't have looked.

And why had he let her have her way? He should have agreed with the coach and persuaded her to go home dirty. But something in her eyes had pleaded with him to help her, to show the coach that she had the same rights as everyone else, and he'd fallen for it. Not only that, but he had to admit that he'd wanted her to have a shower, hoping he would catch a glimpse of her.

Now he wished he hadn't.

Rain Mackenzie was nothing but trouble and he should stay the hell away from her. Then why did he keep doing the opposite? *I must be going insane.*

Chapter Seven

In the bus on the way home, Jesse sat in the very back with his best friend and band mate Zane Jones. Zane had introduced himself as they passed her, while Rain spread herself over the two seats immediately in front of them. She sank down and rested her head against her bag, closing her eyes for a while. Getting up at six a.m. on a Saturday morning wasn't her idea of fun. Although she had to admit she'd enjoyed the game, especially the goal she'd helped score. The less said about the shower incident, the better though ...

Jesse had brought a guitar and was strumming it, picking out a tune. Rain found her foot tapping along involuntarily. It was catchy and had a good beat. She heard Zane say, 'Yeah, that's pretty good. Let's try to come up with some lyrics for that. I've got a pad and a pen here somewhere, hang on.'

Rain heard rustling, then the would-be lyricists got started.

'What should it be about?' Zane asked.

'Temptation,' Jesse said without hesitation, as if it was something he'd just been thinking about. 'How about beginning like this – "*Temptation is a sin, but it's eating me alive, I ...*" er, shit, can't think of anything that rhymes with that.'

'Drive? Thrive? Uhm ... strive?'

'Not good. Think again.'

Rain listened as the two of them argued for a while, trying to come up with a line that rhymed with Jesse's, but their suggestions became more and more ridiculous. They tried to begin the song in some other way, but got stuck once again. The sentence he'd first come up with kept bouncing around her own head though, and she could think of loads of ways to continue it. In fact, now that he'd got her started, she felt she could probably write an entire poem about temptation. The truth was she was suffering from it herself. Images of Jesse's abs kept flashing in and out of her mind and she really wished she hadn't seen him half-naked. There was no way she would forget that in a hurry and that was incredibly annoying.

Finally, she couldn't stand to listen to the two of them bicker any more, so she sat up and glared at them. 'For God's sake, don't you guys ever write poetry in English class?'

They stopped in mid-sentence and stared at her. 'What?'

'Poetry? Are you kidding?' Zane looked vaguely disgusted as if that was something only weirdos did.

'Song lyrics are a kind of poetry,' Rain said impatiently. 'Give me that and shut up for five minutes. I'll write your damned song for you.' She practically snatched the pad out of Zane's hand and he was so surprised that he handed over the pen without a word. Rain bent over the paper and started to write, the words pouring out of her in a furious torrent.

Temptation is a sin, but it's eating me alive
Like a snake inside my brain, don't think I will survive
Another night of torture, please leave me alone
You're scaring me you know, my head is not my own

Temptation is like tentacles, they're pulling me apart
It hit me when I saw you, right from the start
Can't stop my thoughts from yearning, always returning
To the one thing I can't have, help me now I'm burning

You tempt me, you tease me, when I look into your eyes
But you belong to her – something inside me dies

Why did this have to happen, it's just so unfair
The world is full of people, but I don't really care
About anyone but you, and I'm sure you'll understand
If I say I want no other, I am yours to command

You tempt me, you tease me, I look into your eyes
But you belong to her – something inside me dies

Your gaze is pure temptation, though I already know
It's not meant for me, and my veins feel cold as snow
When I think what could have been, but now never
    will be
Can't help but wonder, do you ever think of me?

Don't tempt me, don't tease me, don't look into my eyes!
I'm leaving, forever, my heart is in disguise
Temptation is a sin, I can't let it win
Just leave me be, don't listen to my cries

At that point she ran out of steam and took a deep breath. She read it through and crossed out '*you belong to her*' and substituted it for '*you belong to him*' since it was going to be sung by a guy, then almost threw the pad at Zane. He held it up so he and Jesse could read it at the same time, their eyes growing wide.

Jesse whistled softly. 'Wow, you're good at this. Real good!' He looked up and straight into her eyes and Rain had to turn away from the intensity of his gaze. She felt as if he'd seen into her soul and that was the last thing she wanted. She wished she'd stopped to think before giving him what she'd written. He was sure to realise that she'd been expressing her own feelings. *Damn.* Now she felt like a complete idiot.

'Holy shit,' Zane added. 'Where did all that come from?'

'I don't know,' she lied. 'It's just a stupid poem. I write them all the time. If it's not the sort of thing you're after, just throw it away.' Rain lay down across the two seats with her legs hanging over the end and closed her eyes.

'No way. We're using this,' Jesse said. 'And you'll get the credit for the lyrics. If we ever get signed, you'll get royalties.'

'Don't worry about it, keep them.'

'Well, if you ever feel like writing some more, just let me know. I'm good at coming up with tunes, but crap at the words.'

'Forget it. I like to keep my poems private.'

'Okay, okay, I was just saying …'

'Well, don't.'

Rain kept her eyes closed, too embarrassed to look at Jesse or Zane again. No way was she baring her soul to them a second or third time. They could write their own stupid lyrics, she thought grumpily.

They began to sing the words she'd written and she had to admit they sounded good when added to Jesse's music. She thought he might just have a hit there. She hoped so, for his sake.

By the time the bus finally arrived back at Northbrooke, Rain knew the new song off by heart. In fact, it was stuck in her brain and she couldn't get rid of it. Irritated with both herself and the guys, she grabbed her kit bag and headed off in the direction of the parking lot, pulling out her mobile to call her parents so they would come and fetch her.

'Hey, Rain, wait up.' Jesse came up behind her and she stopped to face him.

'What?'

'Do you need a ride? I've got my car over there.' He nodded towards a beautiful metallic-blue Ford Mustang convertible parked nearby.

'That's yours? Wow, I didn't know you had a 1967,' Rain said without thinking.

Jesse put his head to one side and raised his eyebrows at her. 'You know what model that is? How come?'

'Oh, my dad has one too and he showed me how you can tell. Slightly larger than the '65 and '66 models, exaggerated features, real glass back window instead of plastic, bigger tail lights, convex instead of concave ...' She shrugged. 'He's seriously into cars.'

She didn't tell him that was the understatement of the year. Sir Anthony Mackenzie had an entire garage full of cars and they were his pride and joy. The Mustang was one of his least expensive ones.

'Cool. What colour has he got?'

'Red. I think I like yours better actually, but don't tell him I said that.'

'So you want a ride or what?'

Rain hesitated, then decided it couldn't do any harm. Besides, it would be a lot faster than waiting around for one of her parents. She was cold and it was still raining. 'Okay, thanks.'

She told him where she lived and he drove off. Rain leaned back into the cream leather upholstery, listening to the lovely roar of the powerful engine, and couldn't help a smile from spreading over her face. 'Sweet,' she muttered appreciatively. 'I think your car sounds even better than Dad's.'

'Thanks. I've done some work on the engine myself.' Jesse seemed pleased that she liked it, but she noticed he wasn't driving to show off, the way some guys did. He took it nice and easy, even if he drove as fast as the speed limit permitted, and he was a good driver.

'How did you manage to afford this? Did your parents buy it for you?' Rain asked.

Jesse laughed, but he didn't sound amused so she guessed this was a sore point. 'No way,' he answered. 'I work part-time at the local garage and I saved up for years. It helped that I was able to do some of the work myself, but it's taken a while to get it the way I wanted.'

'I see. Well, you've done a good job.'

All too soon they were drawing up in front of her parents' house, a large old clapboard mansion that looked vaguely Gothic, with little towers, curly bits of joinery and huge windows. Rain thought it was kind of cool, although she preferred their small manor house in England. This house was situated right on the edge of a forest, which made it seem a bit dark and gloomy, whereas their English home had acres of parkland all around and was light and airy.

Jesse stopped the car and whistled. 'Nice pad,' he commented.

'Yes, it's not bad. Well, thanks for driving me home and … er, thank you for helping me out with the shower thing.' She knew she was blushing again, so she opened the door quickly and started to get out.

'You're welcome. And Rain?'

'Yes?'

'If by any chance you should feel like thanking me a bit more, I really would appreciate a couple of song lyrics. I wasn't kidding, you're good and if our band is ever going to get anywhere, we need great songs so we can send out demos.'

She swallowed a sigh. He was right, she owed him. 'How many?' she asked tersely.

'Well, there are usually ten or twelve songs on an album, but even one more would be great. We can probably manage the rest ourselves.' He sounded hopeful now and she couldn't stop herself from looking at him, although she regretted it almost instantly. His big blue eyes were fixed on her in a very disconcerting way and she had to take a deep breath before answering him.

'Okay, I'll see what I can do.'

'Great, thanks. I appreciate it.'

His smile made her want to write a hundred song lyrics, so she slammed the door shut and legged it to the front door quickly before she made a complete fool of herself. She didn't look back until he'd roared out of sight.

There was one great thing Rain had heard about America – the fact that you could drive when you were only sixteen. She couldn't wait to get a driver's licence, so had made it a priority to apply for one straight away. To her dismay, she found it wasn't as easy to get one as she'd thought. First, she'd have to have a provisional permit for at least six months. Then there was classroom instruction and driving lessons, as well as logging a huge number of hours driving with a relative as tutor. And finally some kind of 'observed driving', with an instructor watching her every move.

'Well, that sucks,' she grumbled to her father. 'I thought it was supposed to be a doddle over here. Everyone in US teen movies is always driving.'

'It used to be, but they've tightened the rules. Makes it safer for everyone.' He smiled at her. 'Don't worry though, I'm sure those six months will fly by. Let's go and practise now, eh?'

Since he was so car mad, Sir Anthony had been very happy to discover a kindred spirit in his older daughter. He had taught her to drive on the small private roads of their English estate long before she was officially allowed to and was very proud of her driving skills.

'You're very good,' he told her, which was praise indeed. 'Much better than your brother, I have to admit.' To his disappointment, Rob had never been terribly interested in cars, much preferring motorbikes instead.

'Thanks, but I'm really disappointed it's going to take so long. I'd been hoping I could drive myself to school so you and mum don't need to give me lifts,' she said. 'I guess I'll just have to get a bike instead.'

'You need a licence for those too.'

'No, I mean bike as in bicycle. Pedal power.'

'Oh, right. Yes, good exercise. Or so I hear.'

Rain grinned. Her father preferred things like squash or tennis in order to keep fit. She'd never seen him ride anything that didn't have an engine.

Later, during dinner, Sir Anthony said, 'At least when you do finally pass your test, Rain, you'll have a choice of cars. You can borrow any one of mine. I know you can drive them all as well as I can.'

His collection of cars was the envy of many of his friends, although he had only brought some of them over to the States, leaving the others behind in England for the time being. Lady Mackenzie called them 'his toys', and the ones currently standing in the garage included some truly stunning sports cars and an old Rolls Royce. Rain was well aware that he'd be doing her a great honour in trusting her with his precious collection, but she also knew she was a good driver and she'd be careful.

'I can't wait! Thanks, Dad!' She circled the table to give him a hug, forgetting everything else for the moment. 'Can I even borrow the Lambo?' she said, trying to sound casual.

Her mother gasped and choked on a mouthful of food. 'Rain, for heaven's sake …'

But Sir Anthony just laughed. 'Why not? It's my old one after all, the new one's not been delivered yet. It would be safe outside your school, wouldn't it?'

Rain beamed at him. 'I'm sure it would be fine. No one would harm such an awesome car, would they? Just in case though, when I do drive it, I'll try to park it right outside the window of the principal's office.'

'Good idea.' Sir Anthony chuckled. 'Wish I could see the faces of the other kids when you turn up in that. Should be fun, eh?' Rain nodded and they exchanged a smile of understanding.

'Anthony, darling, are you sure that is wise?' Lady Mackenzie was staring at her husband as if he'd taken leave of his senses. 'It's so fast. I mean, that's a dangerous car and she'll be seventeen when she takes the test. You know what new drivers are like.'

'It's only dangerous if it's driven by an idiot, and I don't consider Rain to belong to that species.' Sir Anthony looked as though this was his final word on the subject, so his wife just shook her head.

'Well, be it on your head.'

Rain gave him another hug. 'Thanks, Dad, you're the best.'

A week went by and the only highlights were the soccer practice sessions, where she got to hang out with Jesse and Zane and have some fun. The three of them goofed off whenever Coach Rivers turned his back and Rain allowed herself to relax for a while. Since the game, the rest of the team seemed to accept her too, and the coach had stopped looking vaguely harassed every time he glanced at her. In class, she still kept her distance from everyone though, especially Jesse. She'd noticed the evil glares his girlfriend sent her whenever she passed, and she didn't want to mess things up for him.

Rain kept telling herself she didn't want any friends in Northbrooke, but she was soon very bored, especially in the evenings and at weekends. So she spent her time down in her father's garage, lovingly polishing some of the cars. Most of them didn't really need it, but the ones that had been used recently could do with a bit more shine. She started with a Ferrari Sir Anthony used quite a lot and when she'd finished that, she continued with the Lamborghini. She'd tried driving it once and it was a bit like being in charge of an untamed tiger. She smiled to herself. *Dad's right, it's going to be wonderful seeing everyone's faces when I arrive at school in this.*

If only she could do it now. She might not even be here in six months' time, so there was no point thinking about it. Rain sighed and threw down the chamois leather she'd been polishing the car with. *Sod it! I want to drive it to school now.*

So why don't you? a little voice inside her goaded. *It's not as if you're not in trouble already. What does it matter if you get grounded here? You never go anywhere in any case.*

Rain stopped and frowned. That was all true. And she wouldn't harm the car, even her father had said so. He trusted her to drive it properly. *Yes, I should totally do it!*

She knew her father was due to go away for a couple of days on a business trip, leaving the following morning. *So all I have to do is fool Mum somehow.* Could she do it? Dare she do it?

Hell, yes! What have I got to lose?

Chapter Eight

Fate played into her hands with a vengeance. The next morning as Rain was getting ready for school, her mother didn't come down for breakfast as usual, so she went to see what was up.

'Are you okay, Mum?' Rain peeked into her parents' bedroom and saw that all the curtains were still drawn. 'Are you sick?'

'Migraine,' her mother muttered. 'Can't stand the light and it hurts.'

'Oh, no! Shall I take a day off from school and look after you?'

'No, please, just leave me in peace.'

'Okay, if you're sure? Can I get you anything before I go?'

'No, thank you. Just need to rest.'

Rain went downstairs again and headed for the garage to get her bike out. Once inside, her gaze fell on the Lambo and it was as if it was calling out to her. *Today! Why not today? Who would ever know? I'll have it back before Mum notices.*

I shouldn't. It's illegal. But she knew she could drive and why would anyone stop her if she kept within the speed limit? *And it would so help make life less boring, at least for one day.* It wasn't long before she set off in the sleek black Lamborghini, making sure she didn't rev the engine too much and thereby alert her mother to what she was doing.

It felt very strange to be driving on the wrong side of the road; whenever she'd practised in England she'd stuck to the left even on the tiny estate roads. Sir Anthony had bought this car in the States so it was set up for driving on the right.

That meant Rain also had to change gears with her right hand, which was just plain weird, although she got the hang of it after a while. *Whoa, this is fantastic!* She whooped out loud, smiling to herself. She was hoping to make a huge impression at school. Not that she really cared what anyone thought, but it would be fun to see their jaws drop.

She wasn't disappointed. A group of boys immediately came to cluster round her the minute she'd finished parking, asking questions and begging her for rides, which she refused. Cody was one of the first, still trying to charm her with that fake smile of his, but Rain told them all to get lost. She admitted to herself that she was seriously frustrated though. The one guy she really wanted to see wasn't there.

In fact, Jesse didn't come to school all day that Monday, which was a bummer in more ways than one. Rain had been working on lyrics for him since last Saturday, and she was ready to show him what she'd come up with. She had tried to write about things that would be relevant to him, such as partying, rocking out and going crazy in general. But although she managed to write some fairly decent lines, the best ones were the lyrics where she let her own feelings speak.

She wrote one about being madly in love, one about feeling blue and another about being misunderstood, but she was particularly pleased with some lyrics about being tempted by the dark side, the bad part of her personality that wanted to do all the things she shouldn't. Like try and tempt Jesse away from his vapid girlfriend, although she didn't write that of course. She let this all out in the lyrics but killed such thoughts in real life. Jesse wasn't for her, and besides, she wasn't sticking around for long anyway.

By the end of the school day, Rain was thoroughly fed up. Home Ed had been massively tedious without Jesse there to cook with, and the soufflé she'd attempted had been a complete failure. *Sodding eggs have to sodding collapse, just when I don't want them to!* And all her other classes had been mind-numbingly boring as well. She'd been told off several times for not paying attention and threatened with detention for a piece of missing homework and for chewing gum. Who cares, she wanted to shout, but kept her mouth shut. Not only that, but her stunt with the shower seemed to have suddenly become known to the entire school and she was getting very tired of guys leering at her and making stupid comments.

'Hey, English, want to come and take a shower with me? I'd do a great job with the soap.'

'Yeah, water massage is my specialty, baby.'

'No, let me. I'll get you real clean.'

'Get lost! And for your information, the word is "speciality",' she said. 'Jeez, can't you people speak English?' That just made them laugh even more, though.

Cody was one of the first ones to try this and she could only marvel at how thick-skinned he was. Somehow she managed to answer without punching him. When she was asked more or less the same question for at least the tenth time, however, she turned to the idiot who'd said it and almost snarled at him. 'I wouldn't shower with you if you were the last guy on earth. Got that?' She looked around. 'And not with anyone else either. I'd probably die laughing at the sight of you guys naked.'

That shut them up, although she was fairly sure they'd still keep talking about her behind her back. *But at least then I don't have to listen to it.*

She just wanted to go home and sulk and decided to skip soccer practice. It wouldn't be any fun without Jesse anyway. When Mrs Langan stopped her in the corridor outside the principal's office, she nearly shrugged the woman off and walked on. Courtesy, which had been instilled in her almost from birth, forced her to stop though. 'Yes, Mrs Langan?'

'Am I right in thinking you know Jesse Devlin?'

'Yes. And?'

'He was absent today and his physics teacher asked me to call him and let him know they're having an important test tomorrow, but I can't get through. Seems the phone's been cut off. I wondered, would you mind stopping by his house on your way home to tell him? I'd be very grateful. You have a car, right?'

Rain frowned. The last thing she wanted to do was go to Jesse's house. 'Doesn't he have a mobile?'

'A what?'

Rain sighed. 'A cell phone.'

'That seems to be switched off too.'

'Well, can't one of his friends take him the message?' Rain didn't understand why Mrs Langan was asking her. 'We're not exactly best buddies.'

'I'm sorry, but you're the first person I saw and I really don't have time to go hunting for anyone else right now. I'm late for a hospital appointment as it is.'

Rain noticed for the first time that the woman had her coat on and was tapping one foot impatiently. 'Oh, all right, then, but I don't know where he lives,' she said.

Mrs Langan thrust a piece of paper at her. 'This is his address and I've written down directions of how to get there. Thank you so much, I really appreciate it.'

Before Rain could say anything else, the woman was gone. Rain stared after her and wondered if she should go and find one of Jesse's friends or even Amber, but then some devil prompted her to do as she'd been asked. She had to admit she was curious to see where he lived and she also wanted to know why he'd been off school. *Skiving?* Clutching the piece of paper, she headed for the Lambo.

A group of boys were still admiring it and several pleaded to be allowed to take her on dates so that she'd let them have a ride, but she shook her head. She wasn't interested in any of them, especially if they were only dating her for the sake of a stupid car.

'Losers,' she muttered to herself.

It took her a while to find Jesse's house, and when she did she was a bit dismayed. It was in a rundown area and the house itself was dilapidated with an air of neglect hanging over it, besides being quite a small bungalow with a messy front porch. It didn't look like anyone had cut the grass on the pocket-sized lawn within living memory. She parked the car outside and went to ring the bell, wondering if this was really such a good idea after all. She should have just tried to find Zane or another of Jesse's friends.

Nothing happened at first, so she rang the bell a second time and finally heard footsteps approaching.

'Who is it?' came a voice from inside.

'Rain Mackenzie. Is Jesse there, please?'

The door opened a fraction and Jesse himself peered out. At least, Rain assumed it was Jesse, although she almost jumped back at the sight of him. He had a black eye and a split lip, and there was blood clotted on his forehead and in little dried rivers down one cheek. He was wearing a T-shirt that was liberally covered in blood stains as well, as were his tracksuit trousers. He tried to scowl at her.

'Jesus, Jesse, what happened?' she blurted out, blinking at him in disbelief.

'Nothing. What do you want?' He didn't sound very friendly today, but now that she was here, Rain decided she'd better deliver her message.

'I ... er, was sent by Mrs Langan to tell you that you have a very important physics test tomorrow apparently. Here are the details.' She held out the piece of paper to him and he snatched it out of her hand with an impatient sigh.

'Do I look like I give a shit about physics tests? Or school, for that matter?' he growled.

'No.' That was the truth, so she couldn't really say anything else. 'Do you want me to help you clean that up?' She indicated his forehead, which looked like it could do with disinfecting at the very least.

'No. Just go away.' He started to shut the door and she realised he was probably embarrassed that she'd caught him looking like this, although she had no idea what was going on or why he was in such a state. Acting on pure instinct, she stuck her foot out to stop him closing the door.

'Please, Jesse, let me help you?'

'I said no.' He peered round the door as if making sure there was no one else there and suddenly caught sight of the Lamborghini parked on his drive. His one good eye opened wide. 'What the hell ...? Is that yours?'

'No, it's my dad's, but he let me borrow it,' she lied.

'You have got to be kidding me.' Jesse opened the door a bit more and just stared at the car. He'd obviously forgotten about his wounds for the moment and Rain was glad of the distraction. 'Is he nuts?'

She laughed. 'No, actually. I'm a good driver and he trusts me not to ruin it.' At least that was the truth. 'I took it to school today. You should've seen the guys drool. It was hilarious.'

'I bet.' He looked at her again. 'Did you let anyone go for a ride?'

'No way.'

'I guess your dad wouldn't like that, huh? Shame. I'd have loved to go in it just once.'

'You can if you want to.'

'What? But you just said ...'

Rain smiled at him. 'I don't mind giving *you* a ride. At least you're not trying to bribe me with a date.' She snorted. 'As if I'd go out with someone who was only interested in me for the sake of my dad's car. Honestly, what do they take me for?'

Jesse smiled back, a bit lopsidedly. 'Bunch of dirtbags,' he agreed.

Rain grew serious again. 'But I'll only take you if you let me clean your face up first.' He started to look mulish again, so she sent him a warning glare. 'I'm serious, Jesse. It could get infected.'

'Like anyone cares,' he muttered, but added, 'Oh, all right. Wouldn't want to mess up the car either. You'd better come in.'

She followed him into a dark hallway, which was clean but dreary. Jesse pointed her in the direction of the kitchen. 'I'll just get changed and bring some antiseptic and stuff. Wait in there, but be careful.'

Rain almost gasped out loud when she entered the kitchen. It looked as if an epic battle had been fought in there, with bits of glass strewn all over the floor and the furniture overturned. One chair was missing a leg and there were pieces of smashed crockery in the sink. She was appalled.

In one corner stood an old broom and almost without thinking she grabbed it and started sweeping the bits of broken glass into a neat pile. At least that way no one would cut their feet, she thought.

'Leave that,' Jesse said harshly from behind her. 'I want the bastard to clean up his own mess this time. I'm done with doing it for him.'

'Who? What's going on here?'

'My dad.'

'What? I don't understand.'

Jesse sighed and righted a chair before sitting down on it. 'He gets drunk every night and sometimes he gets violent. Usually I stay in my room with the door locked, but when I came out this morning, he was having a "hair of the dog" which set him off again. I don't think he'd sobered up much from last night. We ... er, had a fight.' He smiled a little sadly. 'I have a feeling he looks worse than me though. I'm bigger than him now, although the alcohol makes him strong.'

Rain sucked in a hissing breath. 'Damn,' she whispered. 'Has this happened before, then?'

'Yeah, lots of times. My mom died when I was ten and that's when he started drinking. He beat me regularly after that, whenever he could find a reason.' He shrugged. 'I'm used to it, but I don't like going to school looking like this.'

'No, I can see why.'

'I'm telling you, the minute I turn eighteen I'm out of here. He can't stop me.' Jesse had his fists bunched and Rain could see he was dead serious.

'No, I don't suppose he could. Right, give me the antiseptic, then.'

She started to clean him up and although he had a nasty cut on his forehead, most likely from a broken bottle, it was only bleeding sluggishly now because she dislodged the scab. Once she'd disinfected it, she put a couple of plasters over it to keep the edges together tightly. 'That should do,' she muttered. 'I don't think you need stitches and you'll soon be pretty again.'

'Pretty?' He sounded aghast and she grinned at him.

'Isn't that what you want to be? Your band will need a pin-up to attract the girl fans and it sure as hell isn't going to be Zane.'

He had to smile at that. Zane wasn't ugly, but he wasn't good-looking either. Most of the time he looked like he'd been dragged through a hedge backwards and his hair was pretty much untameable. 'So are you done? Can we go for a ride now?'

She gave an exaggerated sigh. 'Yes. I do so love being popular. I should have tried driving that thing earlier.'

He punched her on the arm, although only in a joking manner. 'You know I don't like you for your car,' he said, and headed for the front door. Rain followed and managed not to ask him if he really did like her, and if so, for what, then?

'Where shall we go?' she said when he'd finished admiring the car from the inside.

'How about the old disused air field outside town? You could drive a bit faster there.'

'Okay. You'll have to tell me the way since I have no idea where that is.'

It proved the perfect place for testing the Lambo's cornering ability and speed. Jesse whooped with delight and was almost speechless with joy when she allowed him to drive the car himself. 'Are you sure your dad won't mind?'

'He'll never know unless you crash it, so take it easy, okay?'

She was a bit worried, but he did drive carefully, although it was Rain's turn to hold on for dear life. Finally, as it was beginning to grow dark, she took the steering wheel again and they headed back into town, stopping to put some petrol in the car to replace what they'd used up. She drew up outside his house and killed the engine.

'Thank you so much, that was totally awesome,' he said, bending over to give her a hug. 'I owe you one.'

Rain was glad it was almost fully dark now since she could feel her whole face burning. 'No you don't, we're quits. In fact, I almost forgot ...' She retrieved her bag from behind her seat and took out the song lyrics she'd written for him. 'Here, these are for you to thank you for last week. Now we're definitely even.'

He glanced at the papers and flicked through them. 'Wow, you wrote some more? Thanks, Rain. Seriously, thank you.'

'Don't thank me until you've read them. It's probably complete bollocks, but it's the best I can do. If I think of anything else, I'll let you know.'

'Bollocks?' He laughed. 'Right, I'd better go in.' He hesitated, as if he wanted to say something else but didn't know how. 'About this ...' He pointed to his battered face and Rain understood what was bothering him.

'It's okay, don't worry. I won't tell a soul. I swear.'

'Good. Well, thanks again. You made my day.'

He left, closing the door of the car with great care and waved once before disappearing inside his house. Rain sighed and started up the engine.

Why was life so complicated?

Chapter Nine

It got worse. When she had driven the car carefully into the garage and parked it in its allotted space, she got out and turned to find her father standing by the door with his arms folded across his chest.

'Hello,' he said, but his eyes didn't have their usual twinkle.

'Dad!' Rain's stomach did an uncomfortable somersault and settled into a ball of tension. She didn't know what to say, so the only obvious word she could think of came out. 'Er, sorry.'

'I should think so too.' He shook his head. 'I trusted you, Rain.'

She hung her head. 'I know. I didn't hurt it in any way, I swear.'

'It's not the car I'm worried about! It's the fact that you deceived your mother *and* drove a car without a licence. Do you know what would have happened if the police had stopped you? Did they stop you? God, I hope not.'

She shook her head, although she could guess, of course, what they would have said.

'At the very least, you'd have lost all chances of getting a licence any time soon. What were you thinking?'

Rain could feel tears threatening and tried to blink them away. 'I don't know,' she whispered. 'I guess I wasn't.'

'Damn right, you weren't!' He sighed. 'You were so lucky not to be stopped. That car isn't exactly inconspicuous, is it? Honestly, what am I going to do with you?'

'I won't do it again, I promise! I just wanted to show off to all those jerks at school.'

Sir Anthony hesitated for a moment, then nodded. 'Very

well, but that was your last chance. I'm not putting up with any more nonsense, understand?'

'Okay. Does … does Mum know?'

'No, she's still sleeping. The rest of my trip was cancelled, and when I came home and found the car gone, I waited. And before you ask, no I won't tell her. There's been enough strife already.'

'Thank you, Dad.' Rain knew she didn't deserve his kindness and it made her feel even worse than she already did.

'Obviously you're grounded though. Indefinitely. Any time you're not in school or at soccer practice, you come straight home.'

She nodded as that was only to be expected. 'But won't Mum ask about that?'

'I'll tell her you've been cheeky once too often or something and I'm fed up with it. She's been telling me you should have been grounded from the moment you got here.'

'Okay.' She swore to herself that she'd be good from now on.

Rain was just coming out of a toilet cubicle after lunch the following day when Amber Lawrence walked in, followed by a group of her friends. Instead of ignoring Rain, the way she normally did, the girl walked straight up to her and put her hands on her hips, looking a bit like a small, angry cat.

'What's this I hear about you driving with my boyfriend? Not to mention taking showers with him? You keep your hands off, you little slut, or you'll be sorry.'

Rain ignored Amber and walked over to wash her hands.

'Are you deaf, Ice Girl? I'm talking to you.' Amber's voice had risen several decibels, so even if Rain *had* been deaf, she would have heard her for sure. It annoyed her that the girl was using Jesse's nickname for her, as if he'd called her that in front of all his friends and not in a nice way. It hurt, although she shouldn't have been surprised. She'd heard other people whisper it too and she told herself she didn't care. *Let them think whatever they want.*

'No, I'm not deaf,' she said, 'but I don't take orders from you so we have nothing to discuss.'

'"I dewn't teak owduhs",' Amber mocked, imitating Rain's British accent while making a stupid face. 'Well, you damn well better this time!'

'Oh, just piss off, will you?' Rain made a shooing motion with her hands, forgetting they were wet, and accidentally flicked drops of water onto Amber's immaculately made up face.

'How dare you?'

To Rain's surprise, Amber flew at her and started to claw her face and pull her hair. It was the archetypal cat fight, the sort of thing Rain hadn't engaged in since pre-school when someone else wanted the toy she had. At first she was so amazed, she just stood there, arms up trying to block her, kind of hoping Amber would run out of steam, but the girl was so worked up it didn't look like she was going to stop any time soon. Rain stepped out of her reach for a moment and held her hands out to ward her off.

'Cut it out,' she commanded. 'I don't want to have to hurt you. I don't fight with people smaller than me.' Amber was at least a head shorter and looked as if she might blow away in a strong wind.

In response, Amber just shrieked something obscene and launched herself at Rain again, this time raining blows with her little fists and grabbing handfuls of Rain's clothing to try and tear it. Rain could see the girl's friends advancing on her as well, and she figured she'd better put a stop to this before things got out of hand. Nearby, she could see two other girls from her Spanish class who were not part of Amber's gang, but she didn't know if they would help her so she decided she was on her own.

'Okay, you asked for it,' she muttered and made fists the way her brother had taught her, not the girly way. She hit out at Amber and managed to time it right so she caught the girl first on the side of the head and then square on the nose. There was a sudden silence, then a scream of pure horror as Amber stopped in her tracks, her mouth and eyes wide open. Blood started to ooze out of her nostrils and it was soon flowing down onto her white strappy designer-label top. She glanced into the nearest mirror, screamed again and clutched her nose, then turned for the door, followed by her cronies, who all threw Rain dirty looks before departing.

The screams could be heard receding down the corridor and Rain assumed Amber would be going to report it to some teacher or other. She didn't care, but just let out her breath in a whoosh of relief that it was over. Fighting wasn't something she normally did, although her brother had shown her how to defend herself if necessary. As she walked back to the sink to inspect her own face in the mirror above it, the other two girls came over. They both looked concerned, although a little wary at the same time.

'Are you okay? Did she hurt you?'

'Not really.' Rain turned her face to inspect each side. 'Just a few scratches. I'll live.'

'I'm sorry, we should have helped you, but …'

'We would have,' the other girl cut in, 'if the others had joined in. Five against one is just not fair.'

Rain gave them a small smile. 'Thanks, I appreciate it.'

'I'm Dakota and this is Hayley,' the girl who'd spoken first said. She was tall and a bit geeky-looking, with limp strawberry-blonde hair, but she had kind eyes so Rain decided not to freeze her out the way she'd done everyone else who had tried to be friendly. The other girl, Hayley, was smaller and slightly plump, with short brown hair falling into a very long fringe that hid almost half her face. She too seemed genuinely nice, so Rain smiled tentatively at them again.

'I know,' she said. She'd learned everyone's names in her classes by now, even if she never spoke to them herself.

'So, er, did you really drive Amber's boyfriend yesterday? Everyone's talking about it because all the guys are, like, so jealous. I hear you apparently had a fabulous car or something?'

'I borrowed my dad's sports car and yes, I did go for a quick drive with Jesse, but I wasn't trying to steal him away or anything. I mean, as if I could! Amber is Miss Perfect, isn't she?'

Dakota made a face. 'She sure as hell thinks so.'

'Unfortunately, so do all the guys,' Hayley sighed. 'Us ordinary mortals have to be content with her leftovers.'

Rain knew she shouldn't discuss this, but curiosity got the better of her. 'So has she dated a lot of guys, then?'

'Yeah, at least six different ones since the beginning of sophomore year, but I think she always had her sights set on Jesse. He was harder to get than the others, but that made her more determined.'

'Smart guy, or so we thought until he fell for it too,' Hayley said. 'I suppose he can't help it though. She just flutters her eyelashes and they all go nuts. It's pathetic really.'

Rain smiled. 'That's guys for you. A pretty face and some obvious curves and they're hooked. Nothing we can do about it.'

Dakota looked at her in surprise. 'Well, you shouldn't have any problems, then. You're stunning.'

'Me? No way. I've been called "the blonde giraffe", "daddy longlegs" and all sorts of things. Most boys find me intimidating because I'm too tall.' Rain sighed. 'I did have a boyfriend back in England called Milo, but he turned out to be a jerk. Anyway, nice talking to you, but I'd better go, I've got class in five minutes.'

'Come sit with us at lunchtime if you want,' Dakota offered, still with a slightly wary expression in her eyes as if she wasn't sure whether Rain would be offended. 'I mean, only if you feel like it.'

'Thanks, I might do that.' Rain was getting kind of tired of being alone all the time and her parents hadn't shown any signs of relenting and sending her back to England. If she had to stay here for any length of time, it might be better to have someone to hang out with.

In the doorway she almost collided with Mrs Langan, who grabbed her arm none too gently. 'Not so fast, Miss Mackenzie,' she said. 'The principal wants to see you.'

Rain just nodded and allowed Mrs Langan to frogmarch her down the corridor, although she shrugged out of her grip as soon as she could.

'I can walk by myself, thank you,' she muttered. She should have known she hadn't heard the last of this.

'Rain? Do you want us to come with you?' Dakota called after her, but she shook her head. She could deal with this on her own.

'Fighting?' Dr A said when she faced him across his desk. 'Didn't think that was still taught at English boarding schools. What was it they used to call it?'

Rain knew he was being sarcastic, but she replied anyway. 'Pugilism? Fisticuffs? And no, it's not usually taught anymore, but self-defence is.'

'Self-defence, was it?' He was frowning, but didn't look massively angry, so Rain wasn't sure quite whose side he was on. Surely he could see the scratches on her face? A couple of them had looked pretty nasty.

'When you're being attacked five to one, yes,' Rain insisted. 'But by all means, punish me for it. I don't care.'

'Hmm. So you don't deny you hit Amber?'

'No, why should I? Although, as I said, she hit me first. Or tried to.' Rain snorted, remembering Amber's puny efforts.

'She has witnesses who say it was an unprovoked attack.'

'Yeah, I bet she does.'

'How about you? Anyone who can speak for you?' Dr A looked as if he really wanted to give her the benefit of the doubt, which she supposed was nice of him, but she decided not to involve her two new friends. They might get into trouble with Amber and her group and that was something Rain didn't want to bring on them.

'No,' she said curtly.

'That's your last word?'

'Yep.'

Dr A sighed. 'Okay, young lady. Two hours of detention on Friday after school. Mr Morley's classroom, he'll be supervising you.'

She nodded. 'What about soccer practice?'

'They'll have to do without you.'

'Right.' She suppressed a sigh. 'Can I go now?'

'Yeah, you can go. And I'd appreciate it if this doesn't happen again.'

'That's not up to me,' Rain said, and left.

Jesse didn't go back to school until Friday, because he wanted his bruises to fade first. He didn't think anyone would miss him much and was therefore surprised to find himself surrounded as soon as he arrived and bombarded with questions.

'What happened to you, man? Did you have an accident?'

'Yeah, was it when you went driving with the Ice Girl?'

'You lucky son of a bitch! How come you got to go riding with her in the Lamborghini and we didn't?'

'And what's with your girlfriend picking fights about it?'

Jesse held up his hands. 'Whoa, whoa, slow down. One at a time. What the hell is going on? So I went for a drive with Rain, big deal. We didn't have an accident, I hurt myself at home. And what's this about Amber?' He looked at Zane, who could usually be relied upon to make sense.

'Your girlfriend apparently picked a fight with the Ice Girl because she'd taken you driving, but she got her nose broken so now Rain is going to have detention this afternoon. Two hours.'

Jesse frowned. 'Shit. So that's what Amber meant. She rang me the other day and just kind of screeched down the phone. I told her I was ill and hung up and I haven't heard from her since.'

'Well, you'd better go find her. She's still pissed and her nose is all bandaged up.' Zane sniggered. 'Maybe it won't be so pretty any more, then you'll have to dump her.'

'Don't be a jerk. I'm sure it's not broken. Rain wouldn't do that.'

Zane gave him a strange look, but said only, 'Oh, yeah?'

Jesse didn't have to go far, because Amber was outside by her locker and the minute she set eyes on him, she threw herself into his arms and started sobbing. Big, fat tears rolled down her cheeks – although without damaging her carefully applied make-up he noticed – and she poured out some story of how Rain had attacked her in the girls' bathroom because she was jealous and wanted to take Jesse away from Amber.

Jesse frowned. 'You sure about that?'

Amber stopped crying, as if someone had pushed a button, and glared at him. Although her nose had a big plaster across the bridge of it, there didn't seem to be any swelling and Jesse doubted whether it was truly broken. More like bruised.

'Are you taking her side?' Amber demanded.

'No, I was just asking how you knew that. I mean, is that what she said?'

She cut him off. 'She didn't *say* anything. She didn't have to because it's pretty obvious. Anyway, if you're going to keep defending her all the time, you can forget about us going all the way any time soon.'

'What?' Jesse blinked, stunned by this change of subject. Amber had been vaguely promising him that she might agree to sleep with him when they'd been going out for long enough and he'd proved himself to be 'the one' for her, but he hadn't really expected her to. So far she hadn't even let him touch her below the waist. 'Are you saying you want to …?'

She looked at him sideways from under her long, blackened lashes. 'Well, I had been thinking about it lately, but if I can't trust you not to flirt with other girls, then you're not the kind of boyfriend who deserves a serious relationship.'

'I haven't flirted with anyone,' he protested, although a little voice inside his head muttered 'oh, yeah?' He ignored it. So he'd talked to Rain a bit more than he should and maybe showed her a part of his life no one else knew about, except Zane, but that didn't mean he was interested in going out with her. There was no point if she was leaving soon.

'You'd better not have. You're mine and I don't do sharing.'

'I'm not a possession, for God's sake,' he muttered.

'I know that, sweetie.' She had changed tactics again and was almost purring now, stroking his chest and running her long fingernails downwards. Normally he loved it when she did that, but he was surprised to find that today it just irritated him. 'But you are my boyfriend, right? You agreed to date me exclusively, remember?'

'Yeah, I did,' he admitted, though he was having more and more trouble recalling just why he'd agreed to anything like that. Until he met Amber he'd been a free spirit, never dating one girl more than once or twice in a row. It suited him better, because he didn't like anyone getting too close. With Amber that hadn't been a problem, since she was mostly only interested in herself and never asked much about his life when he wasn't by her side. Now suddenly that seemed wrong. Shouldn't there be more give and take in a relationship?

'Well, then, will you promise me not to go driving with the Ice Girl again? I understand that the fancy car was too tempting even for you, of course it was, but my daddy has promised to buy me a new car soon and I'll let you drive that if you like?'

'Sure, cool. What will you get?' He thought it might be a good idea to steer the conversation into less stormy waters. To his relief, this diversionary tactic worked.

'Oh, I'm thinking about a Corvette. What do you think? Daddy says it's a teensy bit too expensive, but I think I can get him to agree. They're so classy, aren't they?'

Jesse just nodded. After driving the Lamborghini, there was no way he could get excited about a mere Corvette, but of course he couldn't tell Amber that. She'd be mad as hell. As they walked towards the classrooms he let her continue talking, answering with a 'mm-hmm' now and then, but his mind was on other things.

He dropped Amber off at her homeroom then went to his. He caught sight of Rain coming in, but she didn't look at him and he noticed that she went to sit with Dakota and Hayley, two of the nicest girls in the class, even if they weren't noted for their popularity. He was glad she'd made some friends at last, but he kind of wished she'd look his way at least once so he could see if she was okay. There was no way she'd have started a fight with Amber, he was absolutely sure of that, but she was going to suffer for it this afternoon. It didn't seem fair.

A thought occurred to him. This was all his fault. *I should have resisted the temptation to go driving with her, even if she had the coolest car on the planet.* In a town as small as Northbrooke he ought to have known he'd be seen and that it would make Amber mad. That was a no-brainer. So what it all boiled down to was that he was the one who'd screwed up and Rain was paying for it. He made up his mind. The least he could do would be to suffer with her.

That was why, when Mr Aiden asked for their assignments to be handed in, he just shook his head and said, 'I haven't done it.'

'What?' The teacher frowned. 'Mr Devlin, I believe I warned you last time this happened that I wouldn't tolerate any more late assignments.'

Jesse shrugged. 'I've been sick, so I didn't have time,' he said nonchalantly.

'Really? Well, maybe we should give you some time in which to do it, then. You can finish it during detention this afternoon. I'll make sure Mr Morley keeps you there until you're done.'

The teacher turned away as if he was afraid Jesse would try to argue with him, but he had no intention of doing that. He'd got exactly what he wanted.

Chapter Ten

Rain sat down in the detention room and stared straight ahead. She didn't know quite what to expect, but whatever she had to do, it didn't matter. Mr Morley walked in and fixed her with a stern gaze.

'Ah, the new girl,' he said. 'Hadn't expected to see you in here so soon.'

She didn't reply.

'Nothing to say for yourself? Well, good. I'd like you to write a poem on the evils of breaking other people's noses and you're staying here until I'm satisfied that it expresses sincere regret for what you did. Understood?'

Rain sighed and nodded. 'Does it have to rhyme?' she asked, pretending to pout at him. She didn't allow herself to smile at how easy this task would be. Instead, she had to make him believe she was finding it really difficult.

'Uhm, no, doesn't matter.'

She bent her head over her notebook and began by chewing the end of her pencil.

There were a couple of other guys in the room, arguing noisily about whatever task Mr Morley was giving them, and Rain didn't notice Jesse until he slipped into the desk next to her.

'Mr Devlin. Again. How nice to see you. Actually, I'm lying – it's NOT!' Mr Morley shouted the last word. 'Don't you ever learn?'

'Guess not,' Jesse muttered. Mr Morley looked as if he wanted to hit him over the head, but he restrained himself.

'I understand you already have a task to do, so get to it. Unless you want to stay here for the rest of the day, I'd suggest you hurry up and finish it.'

'Yes, sir.'

Jesse rolled his eyes at Rain, who bent forward to hide a smile. It was nice to have him as company; it made her feel less vulnerable somehow.

Mr Morley went to sit at his desk and became engrossed in a book while he chewed noisily on an apple. Soon after, Jesse dropped his pen and had to stand up and come round his desk to pick it up. On the way back to his seat, he stumbled slightly and Rain saw something small and white land in her lap. Without thinking, she covered it with one hand.

'Is there a problem, Devlin?' Mr Morley scowled at Jesse. 'Procrastination never got anyone anywhere.'

'No, sir,' he murmured and sank into his seat, leaning his head on one hand and staring at the sheet of paper in front of him.

When the teacher had returned his attention to his book at last, Rain dared to look down. In her hand, she held a crumpled piece of paper and when she quietly unfolded it, she found a number scribbled there, together with the words 'Txt me now'. She felt in her jeans pocket for her mobile, looked up to check if Mr Morley could see what she was doing, then fished the phone out and sent Jesse a text message.

What's up?

His reply came faster than she'd expected.

Sorry u r here. My fault. 4give me?

She didn't dare look at Jesse, in case she gave the game away to Mr Morley, but under cover of the desk she typed a quick reply.

Not yr fault. Nthing 2 4give. R x

She added the 'x' at the end, even though she knew she probably shouldn't. *But it doesn't mean anything – everyone does it.* And it was just her usual way of signing off. It wasn't a kiss as such. *Not really.* So surely it would be okay? As long as Amber didn't read his text messages and get the wrong idea.

Her phone vibrated again and she thanked her lucky stars she'd remembered to turn the sound off earlier.

4 what it's wrth, I didn't blieve A. She startd it rite?

Rain thought about this for a moment. If she agreed, then she'd be accusing his girlfriend of being horrible and presumably he didn't want to hear that. On the other hand, he seemed to be implying that he knew what she was like. So why was he with her, then? Amber must have some kind of hold over him and she thought maybe she could guess what it was, but she didn't want to think about that.

Yes but dsn't matter. How r songs comin along? R x

She defiantly added the x again, since she figured it would look odd if she didn't now. He obviously wasn't reciprocating, but maybe that was a guy thing? And she decided the change of topic was necessary, since there was no point discussing what had happened any more. It was over with and after today, she would make sure she stayed well away from both Amber and Jesse.

Gr8! Love them all. Thnx again. Will u come n listen 2 us jam Tuesday? Zane's grage, 2pm. & whts the x?

Oh, my god! He's questioning the x? Rain felt her cheeks heat up and bent forward so her hair would shield her face from view. *How the hell do I answer that? Surely he must know what it means? Or maybe they do things differently here?* She knew she still had a lot to learn about American society, but she'd thought this was one of those things that would be the same on either side of the pond. *Shit! What do I do?* Rain was saved from answering immediately as Mr Morley called out, 'I don't hear much writing, people. Get a move on! I don't want to be here all day even if you do.'

She scribbled a few lines of her poem, crossed out some

words to make it look as if she'd struggled to find the right rhymes, then wrote some more. All the time her mind was working furiously, however. What should she reply to Jesse? And why had he asked her to come and listen to them jam? Surely he should be keeping his distance now? *Just like I should.*

He seemed to be concentrating on his homework too, so she couldn't catch his eye. When Mr Morley had become engrossed in his book once again, she dared to text Jesse back.

Why? That's askin 4 truble. & x is a UK thing, just ignore pls

His reply came fairly quickly.

U rote the songs. Hav a rite 2 b there. A goin shoppin all day w mom. Cing hr aftr. x That text was immediately followed by **C – am b ing a Brit**

That made her want to smile and she shot him a glance from under her fringe. He was carefully not looking in her direction, but she saw that his mouth was twitching as if he was trying to suppress a smile too.

Will thnk abt it, she wrote back. **Address? R x**

He texted her the address, followed by another x, which made her feel all kind of warm and fuzzy inside, even though she knew it literally meant nothing to him. Then they both put their mobiles back in their pockets and got on with their work. Mr Morley came around after half an hour or so and despite looking like he was sucking on a sour sweet, he declared that it would do and they could go.

Rain pretended to take a while to pack up her stuff, which was just as well because when she came out she found that Amber had been waiting for Jesse and pounced on him the moment he came out the door. She sent Rain a look of triumph over his shoulder as she snuggled up to him. This made Rain grit her teeth, but she ignored it and just carried on walking. Just before reaching her bike, which was chained up outside the school, she received one last text from him.

C u Tuesday. Pls b there. x

How could she possibly refuse?

She'd forgotten she would see Jesse the next day though, as they had a home game.

'Where were you yesterday?' Coach Rivers barked at her when she arrived at the very last minute and pulled off her tracksuit top, ready to run out onto the field and join in the warm-up exercises. 'And you, Devlin?' Rain looked over her shoulder and saw that Jesse had arrived even later and was standing just behind her.

'Detention,' they said at the same time, then looked at each other and burst out laughing.

'You think that's funny?' The coach was scowling at them. 'Because it sure as hell doesn't seem like it to me! You need all the practise you can get and *you've* missed every session this week.' He pointed a finger at Jesse, then looked at Rain. 'And as for you, girl, I've only seen you once this week. That's not what I call team spirit, people.'

Rain tried to compose her features, even though she still felt like giggling. Not because the coach wasn't right – he was, obviously – but because just being with Jesse made her want to smile. It was crazy. 'Sorry,' she muttered.

'Yeah, we'll do better next week,' Jesse added. 'I was sick.'

'Make sure you do and no excuses.' Coach Rivers nodded towards the field. 'Now get your asses out there.'

They jogged out side by side to join the others and Zane came towards them. 'What was that all about?' he whispered. 'You guys in trouble?'

'Yep, but it doesn't matter. We'll show him today that we don't need to go to every practice session. Right, Rain?'

Jesse jogged on the spot while Rain bent to stretch her hamstrings.

'If he lets us play,' she murmured. Somehow she doubted it.

'He'll have to. He's still got three players injured.' Jesse grinned at her. 'Are you going to pull any more girly stunts today?'

She tried to glare at him but didn't succeed as there was a smile tugging at her mouth that refused to go away. 'No, I'll play by the rules.'

'What are you talking about?' Zane looked confused.

'Nothing,' they said in unison, and again started laughing.

Zane shook his head at them. 'You guys are weird.' He glanced over towards the bleachers, where a small but faithful crowd of supporters had gathered. 'So where's Amber today?' he asked. He sounded casual, but Rain sensed he was worried that her camaraderie with Jesse would lead to more trouble.

'At the mall,' Jesse said and rolled his eyes. 'Again.'

Once the game got under way, Jesse proved to be right. The coach kept him and Rain sitting on the bench for the first half, but after the break the team was losing by two–nil and he had no choice but to send them onto the field to substitute two players who'd been less than useless. 'I sure hope you guys can do better, despite your slacking,' he muttered, which made Rain even more determined to prove that they could.

'I think we might need your eyelashes after all,' Jesse said quietly and flashed her a smile.

'Shut up!' But she knew he was just teasing. 'This isn't going to be easy though. What else can we do?'

'I'll tell Zane to try and kick in some high balls so I can maybe head them into goal.'

'Are you good at headers?' she asked as they made their

way to midfield where the ref was waiting to start them off again.

'Sometimes. Why?'

'Then if we get awarded any corner shots, let me take the ball and I'll try to aim it in front of the goal so you can head it in.' She grinned. '"Bend It Like Beckham".'

'What?' He looked puzzled.

'You know, Beckham is great at corners.'

'Yeah, sure, but what's with the "bend it" thing?'

'Oh, it's a movie about a girl who wants to play like him. She does, too.'

Jesse laughed. 'You think you can pull that off? Guess it's worth a try.'

'I can do it,' she said confidently, although she wasn't totally sure. It was something she'd practised with Rob, but it was hard to get it right every time. Still, as Jesse said, it was worth a try. All they needed was a corner.

At first, it seemed they wouldn't be needing any tactics, because Zane managed to outrun his opponents and score all by himself. But then nothing happened for ages and Rain could see Coach Rivers pacing around with frustration. *If only we could catch a break.*

Five minutes before full time, they got one. Jesse was dribbling the ball very close to the edge of the field to the left of the other team's goal. Rain saw him feint, which had the defender turning round in a half-circle, and when the guy had his back to Jesse, he tried to pass it to Rain, but missed. The ball bounced off the defender and across the line, and the referee blew his whistle.

'Corner!' he shouted.

Jesse threw the ball to Rain and she saw some eyebrows raised among the opposing team members. *I guess they don't think a girl can kick that far. We'll just see about that* ... Swallowing down nervous butterflies that danced inside her stomach, she went over to the corner and placed the ball where Rob had taught her. She hadn't done this for a while, but she knew she could. *Don't think about failure. It's not an option.*

She drew in a deep breath and checked that Jesse was in place near the front of the goal. The defenders were more or less in a group, trying to stop anyone from getting close enough to head the ball, but Jesse was tall and she saw him sticking up behind the others. *If only I can aim high enough, we'll be fine. Right, here goes.* She stepped back, took aim and went for it.

The ball sailed through the air in a perfect arc, exactly as she'd planned, and she saw quite a few mouths fall open in surprise. At the last moment, Jesse jumped. His forehead connected with the ball and it went flying into the goal, just to the right of the goalie who was too late to catch it.

Rain jumped too, punching the air with her fist. 'Woo-hoo!'

The game ended with a draw, which, as the coach muttered, was 'better than losing'. 'Well done, guys, but I don't want to see any more slacking, okay?' he told Jesse and Rain. 'Next week you turn up for practice or you're off the team, goals or no goals.'

'Understood.'

As they headed for the changing rooms, Jesse came up behind Rain and casually draped an arm around her shoulders. 'Great corner, Rain. That was awesome.'

'Your header too.' She smiled at him.

Zane came up on her other side and put his arm round her too. 'So what other secrets aren't you guys sharing?' he asked, sending them a quizzical glance.

'Secrets? That was just team tactics.'

'Yeah, for a team of two.' Zane shook his head. 'But hey, I'm not complaining. You scored a goal, and if you want to leave the rest of us out of it …'

Rain pushed him in a friendly way. 'Cut it out, Zane. You scored a goal all by yourself so you didn't need our help. And as for the corner kick, we were just trying something out. It could have gone wrong.'

'If you say so. I'm glad it worked.'

Rain was too. *If I'd failed, I would have looked like a right prat!* And that was something she definitely didn't want to do around Jesse.

Chapter Eleven

Okay, so I guess I was wrong. Rain hadn't believed it mattered whether she was grounded or not here in Northbrooke, but she now realised it did. A lot. Because having thought about it, she really wanted to go to the jamming session to hear the songs she'd helped to write. As Jesse had said, she had a right to be there. *And he asked me specially.*

Sir Anthony may be a lenient father most of the time, but he'd been surprisingly firm over the Lamborghini incident and Rain didn't think that appealing to him would get him to lift the ban on going out. She knew he meant it and at the time, she'd thought it only fair. Grounding her was probably the least he should be doing and it was only because he was so nice he hadn't stopped her allowance as well.

So she couldn't ask him to let her go out, even if it was just this once.

But I want to go.

There was only one thing to do – lie.

Rain cringed inwardly at the thought. She'd promised her dad she would behave from now on, but this was just so important. *Important enough to risk him getting even more angry?* After some soul-searching, she decided it was. *I have to be there.*

The only question was – what could she say?

'Is it okay if I stay after school today to study with my friends Dakota and Hayley? The teacher is threatening us with a pop quiz some time this week. We might go to Dakota's house.'

'A what? You're starting to sound American, darling.' Rain's mother smiled at her, making Rain feel bad for deceiving her. *But it's not as if I'm going to do anything bad. I'll just be listening to a band in broad daylight.*

Rain protested, 'Quiz is an English word.'

'Yes, but you've always said "exam" before, or "test". You're obviously being influenced by your surroundings.'

'Well, like, it's kind of hard not to.'

Lady Mackenzie's smile faded. 'Don't say "like" every two seconds, please! It's extremely aggravating.'

'Everyone does that back home too.'

'Not with a twang.'

Rain swallowed a sigh. *Who cares how I speak?* 'So can I stay, then?'

'Yes, yes, of course, if it's necessary. Will you take your bicycle? Only I've got bridge this afternoon so I'm not sure when I'll be able to pick you up.'

'No, don't worry, I'll be fine on my bike.'

Rain was glad her father had already left for work. She felt sure he'd have seen through her white lie immediately.

As soon as she got to school, she went to find Hayley and Dakota. She didn't like being beholden to anyone, but they had offered to help her with anything and she was getting to know them a bit better so she was sure they wouldn't mind. They hadn't actually hung out after school yet or anything, but they'd been texting each other on and off and Rain liked their sense of humour. She briefly explained her predicament.

'I need to go somewhere this afternoon, but I'm kind of grounded at the moment, so I told my mum I was going to study with you two. I gave her your mobile number, Dakota, and told her I didn't know your home phone. Is that okay?'

'Sure thing. If anyone asks for you, we'll just say you're in the bathroom and you'll call back. Then we can text you. How's that? Good plan?' Dakota smiled, obviously happy to be part of an intrigue.

'Thanks, that would be great.'

'So where are you going? I mean, if you don't mind me asking.' Hayley grinned at her. 'Big date?'

'Uhm, not exactly.' Rain hesitated. 'Can you guys keep a secret?'

They both nodded, so she told them what was happening, after first checking that no one else was in earshot.

'Wow, that's so cool!'

'Yeah, you are sooooo lucky!'

'You think?' Rain hadn't realised it was such a big deal.

'Of course.' Hayley was almost jumping up and down with excitement. 'Escape From Hell are the best band in the school. There was this competition a while back and they won, like, hands down. They're awesome!'

'Oh, I didn't know. I kind of thought they were only fooling around a bit. Just starting up or something.'

'No way.' Dakota seemed equally excited. 'Just wait till you hear them. They're going to be huge.'

'Yeah, maybe we'll get interviewed one day because we were at school with them.' Hayley laughed. 'Famous by association.'

'Calm down,' Dakota told her friend and punched her lightly on the arm. 'Don't get too carried away, fan girl.'

Rain looked from one to the other and raised her eyebrows. 'Do I detect something here? Hayley, you fancy one of the band members?' she teased.

Hayley turned pink under her fringe, but both she and Dakota giggled. 'No, I don't "fancy" anyone,' she said, imitating Rain's English accent, although in a nice way so she wasn't offended.

'She might have a crush on someone though,' Dakota said, nudging her friend.

'Do not.'

'Do too!'

'And you don't?'

'Okay, okay, so I get the feeling you're both "crushing" on … what were they called?'

'Escape From Hell. Seriously cool name, right?'

'Yeah, I guess.' Rain didn't want to admit that she agreed, but it was a great name for a band. She could already see the headlines in music magazines, who would shorten it to E-Hell or EFH or something, like they turned My Chemical Romance into My Chem or Fall Out Boy into FoB. She gave herself a mental shake. *What's it got to do with you?* 'Well, I'd better go. Thanks again, you guys. I really appreciate this.'

'No problem,' Hayley said. 'Just promise you'll tell us all about it tomorrow, okay?'

'About anyone in particular?' Rain couldn't resist asking.

Hayley said 'No!' at the same time as Dakota whispered 'Drummer'. She got a dirty look for this, but she and Rain both laughed. Rain walked off feeling happier than she had for a while. It felt good to have two co-conspirators. Friends even. Maybe these two wouldn't let her down the way her English friends had done. She instinctively felt she could trust them because they were different. Loyal. If only Milo had been like that … but he hadn't. *There's no point thinking about that. And who cares? I'm going to a jamming session!*

Zane drove her to his house. He'd said that it was probably safer that way, if Jesse wanted to stay in one piece. 'You know what I mean? Hellcats have long claws even if their noses are a bit bruised.' The smile that accompanied these words showed Rain that he was just looking out for his friend.

She understood and she didn't mind. She was just happy to be going.

'So where's the Lambo today?' Zane asked.

'Er, at home. My dad didn't think I should take it to school any more. And after what happened with Amber, I kind of agreed with him.' She shrugged, trying to make out it wasn't a big deal. She hadn't told anyone she didn't have a licence and she'd rather no one found out about that.

'That's a shame. I would have loved to go for a quick ride.'

'I bet. Please don't tell me you're going to ask me for a date just so I'll drive you? It's not going to happen. In fact, I'm never driving it ever again.'

Zane grinned. 'That pissed you off, huh, everyone pestering you for dates? Actually, I was just going to suggest cruising past the burger bar in the centre of town, where everyone hangs out after school. If they saw you driving me too, maybe Amber would lay off nagging Jesse about it.'

'Oh, hell. I didn't mean to get him into trouble.' Rain sighed. 'It was just a spur of the moment thing, you know? I honestly didn't think.'

'I believe you, but I'm not Amber.' He must have caught her anxious expression, because he added, 'Hey, don't worry about it. Jesse's a big boy, he can take care of himself.'

Rain nodded. 'I just don't want to make things difficult for him.' A thought struck her. 'How about you, you have a girlfriend?' She'd never seen him with one, but maybe he was dating someone from another school.

It was his turn to laugh. 'Now you ask, after I drive you halfway across town in my car? As it happens, no, not at the moment, but I'm open to suggestions.' He wiggled his eyebrows at her.

'Thanks, but no thanks.'

He sighed as if she'd broken his heart. 'Can we at least be friends, then? Just so I can ride in your Lambo some time?'

'Maybe.' He made big eyes at her, which made her laugh. 'Okay, I tell you what, if I ever do drive it again, you'll be my first passenger. All right?'

'Really? Sweet!'

Zane lived in a pretty neighbourhood of similar-looking two-storey houses with either huge carports or detached double garages with a room above. Zane's house was the garage kind. When they arrived, Jesse and two other guys were waiting on the drive. And although Jesse raised his eyebrows at them, he didn't say anything. Zane went over and whispered something in his ear and he nodded then smiled at Rain as if he understood her caution in not asking for a ride from him. She smiled back and he introduced her to the two other band members.

'This is Mick, he plays drums, and this is Scott, who's on vocals.'

'Hi.' Feeling a bit embarrassed, since they were looking at her as if they were wondering what she was doing there, she followed them up to the room above the garage. It was set up like a studio, with a drum kit, a guitar, a bass and a couple of microphones, all hooked up to huge speakers and amplifiers with some kind of mixing deck along one wall. *Impressive!* Rain was beginning to see what her friends had been talking about – these guys were serious about their music.

'I have some good news, guys,' Jesse said. 'I've been asked if we can play a sort of mini-concert at school next week, for an hour before the school dance. I said we'd do it, is that okay?' There were nods of agreement. 'Great. The thing is, I know we've practised a lot of well-known songs by other bands, but I thought it was time we had some of our own, and that's where Rain comes in. She's helped me write some new material for us and it would be good if we could learn at least a couple of them before the gig.'

'What kind of songs?' Scott didn't seem too enthusiastic, unlike the other two.

'I'll play them to you, you'll see. I think you'll like them. Listen, okay?'

'Fine, whatever.'

Jesse had the pieces of paper Rain had given him in his hand and spread them out on a stand in front of him. He started strumming his guitar, then launched into song. She knew already from the bus trip that his voice was fairly good, but not outstanding. He'd never make lead vocalist, but he'd be okay as a backing singer, she thought. It was just as well he knew his limitations and had found Scott to do it for him, but for the purposes of teaching the others the songs, he was doing fine.

He started with the 'Temptation' song they'd written on the bus and Zane, who played bass, joined in on that one. Then Jesse continued with some of the others, and Rain was amazed at how good her lyrics sounded when set to his music. It was as if he'd really captured the essence of what she had written. Her exact feelings soared through the room. It made her heart beat faster, the blood sing excitedly through her veins.

'So what do you think?' he asked, when he'd finished.

'Great stuff,' Mick said and Zane nodded approval, but Scott still looked dubious.

'They're okay,' he said, 'but I don't know if I can learn all that in a week.'

'Well, let's just give it a try, all right?' Jesse seemed to be trying his best not to be impatient and Rain wanted to knock Scott on the head for him. Surely it wasn't that difficult? In fact, she could probably sing half the songs herself already, although she did have the advantage of knowing the lyrics.

The band began to practise, warming up with a couple of well-known numbers first, and Rain sat in a corner just enjoying listening to them. The three people on instruments were really good, she thought, playing together in perfect harmony. They must have practised a lot. Scott had a good voice and did okay on the songs he knew, but began to flounder when it came to the new material. After several tries, he mastered most of the first song and then asked for a break.

'I'm just going outside for a smoke,' he said and disappeared.

Zane rolled his eyes at Jesse. 'I wish he wouldn't,' he said quietly. 'It's not going to do his vocal chords any good.'

Jesse shrugged. 'Gives them that deep sound though. And he drinks a lot to make up for it.'

'Too much,' Mick added with a frown. 'Will he be okay to sing, do you think?'

'Yeah, he'll be fine,' Jesse said, but he didn't sound as confident as his words were obviously meant to be. 'What did you think, Rain?' He turned to her and smiled. 'Are we crap or what?'

'No, you're brilliant. In fact, I can't believe how good you are and those new songs sounded great. I'm glad you were able to use the lyrics.'

'Of course, why wouldn't I?' Jesse turned to Mick to explain that Rain had actually written them all by herself.

'Except the first line of "Temptation",' she said with a laugh.

'Yeah, how could I forget?' Jesse grinned at her. 'I was beginning to wish I'd never come up with that when you saved me. Zane couldn't think of a single decent line that rhymed with it.'

'I could so, you just didn't like them,' Zane protested. 'But hey, I'm not proud, I'll admit Rain's stuff is much better than mine, even if it is girly poetry.'

'Watch it, you.' She punched him playfully and he chuckled.

'I'll tell you what though,' Zane added, 'that song about the "Dark Side"? I think we should do part of it like rapping, you know, and then Scott can let rip with the chorus after each verse. What do you think?'

'Hey, that's not a bad idea.' Jesse found the paper with the words. 'Like this?' He started saying the words, while Mick picked up the beat on the drums.

There's a place I shouldn't go and it's deep inside my head
It scares me just to think of it, so dark and full of dread
I know I must suppress even the slightest little thought
Of giving in or giving up – come on, I can't be bought

Zane, whose voice was loud and raucous, belted out the chorus since Scott wasn't back yet.

Did you think that you could tempt me over to the dark
*   side*
Did you think I'd make it easy, not giving you a hard ride
Well you got it wrong, forget it – I'm never giving in
You can try your best, but hey – I'll take it on the chin

The three guys grinned at each other and Jesse played the tune on his guitar with Zane following on bass as Jesse did the next verse.

The thoughts are calling me to come, they're trying to
*   pretend*
That the dark side is just normal, there is nothing to
*   defend*
But I know that's a lie, I'm just not gonna believe
That thinking it is right and will give me a reprieve

They both sang the chorus this time, then jumped straight into the next verse.

The Dark Side is a selfish place for those who just don't
*   care*

About anyone but them and they really aren't aware
That the world is not just theirs and they had better
*   share*
Instead of greed, guys, how about some truth and dare

Did you think that you could tempt me over to the dark
*   side*
Did you think I'd make it easy, not giving you a hard ride
Well you got it wrong, forget it – I'm never giving in
You can try your best, but hey – I'll take it on the chin

The dark side is inside of me, inside of everyone
But me – I'm gonna bury it, I am forever done
With thinking I can have it all, it really isn't true
Life is just shit for most of us, I'll stay forever blue

Scott came back in just as they all launched into '*Did you think that you could tempt me …*'. He frowned at them. 'What the hell is going on? What are you doing?'

The others explained and since it meant him having only the chorus to learn, he agreed to the change. He didn't seem very happy about it though, and secretly Rain thought that Zane's way of singing it had sounded better. But of course she couldn't say that. The band practised some more and it went fairly well, although Rain was itching to help Scott out the whole time since he was having trouble getting the new songs right. She restrained herself and stayed quietly in the background.

They packed up and got ready to go just before five and she stood up too. 'Thanks for letting me listen,' she said to Jesse. 'I'm sure you'll be a hit next week.'

'Will you come and hear us play?' he asked.

'I don't know. I hadn't really planned on going to that dance.' She did not want to tell him she was grounded, especially since she hadn't told him about driving the Lambo without a licence.

'Come on, you should be there so we can give you credit for your part.'

Rain had great trouble saying no to him when he looked at her with those big blue eyes. She felt as if she was drowning in them and her will was slowly being sucked out of her. It was no surprise, then, that she found herself nodding. 'All right, I'll come and listen to you, but I'm not staying for the dance. And please, don't mention my name. It might be better for everyone if you don't.'

He nodded, catching her drift. 'If you say so, but if we ever get signed, your name will be on the record. No arguing about that.'

'Fine.'

'You know, we're going to have to rehearse a couple more times this week and next. Why don't you come and listen again? Thursday maybe?'

'We'll see, depends on homework and stuff.' Rain didn't really care about homework at the moment and obviously the problem was being grounded anyway, but she also wasn't sure she ought to hang around with Jesse and his friends any more. It was tempting though, which was why she hadn't said no outright.

'Think about it, okay?'

'Sure, will do.'

Zane came over to join them. 'So, since we're best buddies now, Rain,' he leaned his head on her shoulder and affected a silly grin, 'want me to drive you back to school to pick up your bike?'

'Best buddies?' Rain gave him a haughty look. 'In your dreams, mate.'

'Mate?' Zane laughed and she pushed him away from her shoulder.

'You just want to show your friends that a girl actually agreed to sit in your old banger, don't you?'

'What do you mean, "old banger"? Are you dissing my car? I'll have you know it's got five hundred horsepower and—'

Rain laughed. 'The hell it does, Zane. More like zero.'

The others were laughing too now, as Zane's car was pretty old and rusty and anyone could see it wasn't exactly the latest model. 'She's got you there, Zane,' Mick said.

Zane shook his head sadly. 'And there I was, trying to do you a favour, Rain. But if you prefer to walk ...'

'No, I was just kidding. It's a lovely car, honest.' Rain smiled at him and he grinned back.

'Okay, let's go, then. Hey, how about I take you to the cinema first? And my finances might just stretch to a pizza afterwards. Or are you busy?'

'Well, I should probably go home, but ... how can I possibly refuse such a generous offer?' Rain laughed again. 'Okay, you're on, but just as friends and I can't be late. Deal?'

'Sure, anything you say.'

Jesse had turned away, so Rain didn't see his reaction to the proposed date, and soon afterwards they all went their separate ways. *Not that it's a real date, since we're just friends, but still ...* She sincerely hoped Jesse wasn't taking Amber to the cinema as well, because she really didn't want to see them together.

Chapter Twelve

Jesse watched his best friend drive away with Rain and swallowed down the hurt he felt. It was ridiculous really. It was nothing to do with him and anyway, she'd made it clear it was only a date with a 'mate', as she'd called him. He knew Zane could be charm personified though and if he set his mind to it, he could probably worm his way into Rain's affections. For some reason, Jesse couldn't stand the thought of that.

Okay, admit it, you want her for yourself. He gripped the steering wheel of his Mustang so tight his knuckles went white.

'No, damn it,' he muttered. He didn't want to complicate his life. Rain was gorgeous, but she was getting under his skin and he wasn't sure he could cope with that. With her, he felt he'd have to give one hundred per cent of himself and he wasn't ready for that kind of relationship. Or was he?

No, far better to keep it simple. *And what am I thinking anyway?* Amber had hinted that tonight was the night they might go all the way, because her parents were out. So why wasn't he excited? Wasn't this what he'd wanted for ages? She'd been putting him off for so long, leading him on, the frustration had built up inside him until he thought he'd explode. But now that he was within sight of his goal, he found himself strangely reluctant to take such a huge step. Perhaps it was because Amber had made it sound as if it was his reward for not so much as looking at Rain all day yesterday. That didn't seem right somehow.

He'd never had this problem before. Girls either wanted to sleep with you or they didn't. Most made you wait at least for a couple of weeks, but not months. Not the girls he'd been out with, anyway. But Amber was different. He'd thought she was special and maybe worth waiting for. Wasn't she?

Surely sleeping with someone shouldn't be a prize for good behaviour? And if she could look at it in such a detached way, then where was the passion, the feeling of being crazy in love and totally carried away?

If he was honest, he didn't want Amber that much either. Not any more.

That thought almost made him stop the car.

Dammit! He was going mad. He must be. 'Forget Rain,' he told himself. *She's leaving soon and you'll be left behind feeling like a complete idiot. Amber will be snapped up by someone willing to give her all the attention she craves and everyone will think you're a loser who couldn't hang onto her.*

He gritted his teeth and made up his mind. He was going out with Amber and that was all there was to it, but he'd tell her *he* wasn't ready to go all the way yet. It was too big a commitment and once she let him do that, he'd be stuck, he was sure of it. She'd never let him go then, and he'd be forever in her debt somehow.

That didn't bear thinking about.

He pulled up outside Amber's house and went to ring the doorbell. She answered it herself, but instead of greeting him with a kiss like he'd expected, she glanced over her shoulder nervously and whispered, 'Sorry, Jesse, change of plan.'

'What do you mean?' He guessed she'd got cold feet again, so it was just as well he'd changed his mind about the whole thing. He felt oddly detached, like it didn't matter at all.

'I got the date wrong. My parents aren't going out tonight, it's next week. They want you to join us for dinner instead.'

'Oh, right.' Jesse was surprised. Her parents had never invited him to join them before. It was almost as if they'd hoped that if they pretended he didn't exist, he'd go away. But he hadn't and maybe they'd finally realised that. 'Uhm, I'm not really dressed fancy or anything.' He looked down at his usual outfit of torn jeans, T-shirt and leather jacket.

'It doesn't matter. No time to go change now anyway, dinner's almost ready.' She led the way into the house. It was one of the new houses that had recently been built on the outskirts of town in a gated community. Huge and a bit too showy, as if the owners had so much money they didn't know what to do with it. As they crossed the cold marble floor of the enormous hall Jesse suppressed a shiver. It was ridiculous to feel intimidated by a house – it was just bricks and mortar after all.

Still, he now had to face its owners.

Amber's parents were waiting in the dining room and as he entered with Amber she whispered to him, 'Daddy wants to talk to you about the Corvette. I told him you know a lot about cars and he wants your opinion. Here's your chance to impress him.'

Jesse took a deep breath before shaking hands with first Amber's mother, then her father. He saw them eyeing his outfit and sighed inwardly. *Maybe this wasn't such a good idea after all.* But Amber must have read his mind, because she murmured, 'It'll be fine,' and led him to a seat.

Each place was set with two knives and forks, two spoons and an extra knife on a small plate to his left. Jesse wondered what he'd need all those for, but then decided Mrs Lawrence was probably just showing off how much silver cutlery she had. She seemed like that kind of woman. There were also three different glasses and a huge napkin. He saw Amber spread that on her lap, so he followed suit. A small, dark woman came into the room with a tray and handed out bowls of soup. She looked Hispanic and was wearing a maid's uniform. *Holy shit,* Jesse thought, *servants. What next?*

'Uhm, not that spoon, sweetie,' Amber purred at him when he picked up a spoon at random to eat his soup with. 'That one's for dessert.'

'Oh, yeah, of course. Sorry, forgot.' Jesse gritted his teeth and grabbed the other spoon, wondering why it mattered as long as he got the food into his mouth without dribbling or something. He made sure he copied Amber after that though, so he wouldn't make any more mistakes, but the whole cutlery thing made him feel deeply uncomfortable.

'So Amber tells me you know a thing or two about cars,' Mr Lawrence said, fixing Jesse with a glare as if he doubted this was the truth.

'That's right. I … er, have some hands-on experience.' He thought it best not to say he worked part-time in the local garage. Being a mechanic would probably seem menial to Amber's dad.

'Uh-huh. She's been bugging me about buying a Corvette and I have to admit they're nice little cars, but I'm not willing to shell out for a brand new one, so I was thinking second hand. What do you say?'

'Sure, why not? There should be some good ones, careful owners and all that.'

'The thing is, I've already found this guy down in Boston who's willing to sell me his and he says he'll give me a good price.' He named the sum and Jesse's eyes widened.

'I'm not sure that's the going rate—' he started to protest. Mr Lawrence was being ripped off, royally. Jesse was interrupted in mid-sentence.

'Oh, he told me most people will pretend they're selling for less, but no one ever does, so I reckon I'd be getting myself a good deal.' Mr Lawrence seemed so sure about this, Jesse didn't dare argue with him. Besides, it wasn't his problem how the guy spent his money, so he kept his mouth shut and just nodded.

'And what do you drive?'

'A 1967 Ford Mustang convertible,' Jesse said, glad that he didn't have to be ashamed of his car at least.

'Not bad, I guess, if that's the kind of thing you like.' Mr Lawrence sounded as if a Mustang was a cheap toy, which made Jesse want to protest, but one look at Amber made him swallow the words. She was shaking her head ever so slightly and he guessed it wasn't a good idea to argue with her dad about anything.

The next course was brought in by the maid and Jesse almost got up to help the woman since the tray she was carrying seemed so heavy. No one else was bothered, however, so he stayed in his seat.

'I hope you like *coq au vin*, Jesse?' Mrs Lawrence gave him a fake smile.

'Sure, I eat everything,' he said, although he wasn't actually sure he wanted to eat cock of anything. Apparently that wasn't the right answer either though since it made Mrs Lawrence grimace. The stuff that was put in front of him looked just like plain old chicken to him, but he didn't want to say so. If she wanted to call it something snobby, that was up to her.

After that, the dinner conversation stayed firmly on topics that didn't interest Jesse at all, like politics and all the Lawrence's rich friends and neighbours, none of whom he knew. He felt like the village idiot, too stupid to be included, but he did his best to look interested and nod from time to time. He made it through the meal, but he drew a sigh of relief when it was over and swore to himself he'd never sit through that kind of thing again, no matter what Amber said. From now on, he'd stay away from her house at mealtimes.

Rain had a good time with Zane, who didn't seem too bothered when she made it quite clear she really wasn't interested in him as boyfriend material. They watched a film, had pizza and spent the whole time arguing good-naturedly about everything under the sun, a bit like she did with her brother, Rob. It was fun but it wasn't serious. And to her relief, her mother didn't comment on the fact that she came home so late. The heavy bag she carried, crammed full of books, must have convinced her she'd been studying.

Phew!

During the next couple of days, Zane often appeared at her side and they continued where they'd left off, their banter making them both laugh. Because he was a nice guy, he also included Dakota and Hayley whenever Rain was sitting with the two of them. And although they were a bit nervous around him at first, they soon relaxed and even dared to flirt with him a little.

'He's kind of cute, don't you think?' Dakota whispered to Rain, then blushed. 'I mean, in a messy sort of way.'

Rain had to laugh at that. The word messy could have been invented for Zane, but the rumpled look suited him to perfection and if she looked at him critically, she had to admit he had a certain charm. He just didn't appeal to her, but that wasn't his fault.

'Yes,' she replied. 'Do you want me to ask if he'll take you out on a date?' She felt fairly confident that Zane would. He didn't seem to mind who he went out with, as long as it was a female. He wasn't serious about anyone, ever, from what she could see, but that didn't mean he couldn't fall for Dakota given half a chance.

'Oh, no, that would be too embarrassing for words.' Dakota looked horrified, so Rain didn't pursue the matter, but she resolved to sound Zane out at the first opportunity.

A week passed quickly, the only real highlights being the soccer practices, which Rain was really enjoying now, and the Monday Home Ed lesson when she and Jesse had fun as usual. They learned how to cook *ratatouille* and although Jesse paid more attention this time, he had a hard time learning how to pronounce that word.

'Guess you can't say my real name either, then,' Rain teased, and rolled her *r* perfectly. 'Reine.'

He smacked her behind with a towel. 'Stop being such a know-it-all. I bet I know lots of car parts you've never heard of.'

She fended him off, trying to wrench the towel out of his hands. 'I guess you're right,' she conceded. 'But leave my bum out of the discussion.'

'"Bum"?' he teased.

'Okay, "butt", then. Who cares what it's called?' She finally managed to pull the towel out of his hands and smacked him back. 'How about *derrière*?'

He rolled his eyes. 'That just sounds really stuck-up, like "rah-tah-touye". And why would I need to pronounce it? As long as I can cook it so it's edible, that's good enough for me. It's just vegetable stew, for God's sake! As for your name, I like Rain better. It suits you. It's cool, like you.'

'Er, thanks, I think?'

Neither Amber nor any of her friends were in that class, so they were able to joke around and talk without anyone reporting back to her, but that was a one-off. The rest of the time, Amber had him on a tight leash. Rain tried not to let it bother her. It was his problem after all.

Thursday had come and gone and Rain decided to give the band rehearsal a miss. Going to that would just be asking for trouble. But on the following Tuesday Jesse came up behind her when she was standing by her locker and whispered, 'Since you missed Thursday, will you come this afternoon?'

She looked up, wondering how to say no without offending him, but he didn't give her the chance.

'Come on,' he said. 'We don't bite, you know that, and

Amber is studying for an exam with some of her friends so she won't know. Just come for a while, please? It might be the last time we can rehearse this week because I've got to work at the garage on Thursday.'

Rain wondered why he wanted her there. 'I don't know. It's not like you need me,' she stalled. *And what will I tell Mum and Dad?*

'Yeah, we do. In fact, if you're there, maybe Scott won't dare grumble so much about learning the new songs. You wouldn't believe how difficult he's being. We tried again over the weekend after I called an extra practice session and it didn't go too well. You wrote them though, and if you're watching he can't say that he thinks they're crap.'

'Why would he think that? They're good.' Rain realised what she'd just said and tried to backtrack. 'I mean, your music is good, the lyrics could be anything.'

He grinned. 'Oh no, you said it, they're good, and you wrote them.'

'Just some stupid poems,' she muttered.

'They're not stupid. I think they capture the mood of most people I know exactly. Please won't you come for just a while?'

What the hell, I'll have to tell my parents I'm revising again.

'All right, then, but I can't stay long.'

'Great, I'll see you at Zane's house in a while.'

She noticed he didn't ask if she wanted a ride, but she knew why. And he was gone before she could change her mind so she closed her locker with a sigh. Why couldn't she say no to him?

Chapter Thirteen

Jesse watched Rain come into the garage room and take a seat. Out of the corner of his eye he saw Scott frown, but of course the guy couldn't say anything in protest. Rain had every right to be there. It almost felt like she was part of the band.

'Hey, Rain, you made it.' Jesse walked up to her and she smiled at him.

'Yep. Can't wait to hear how far you've got.'

He made a face and whispered, 'Not as far as I'd like, but you'll hear that for yourself soon enough.'

'Scott?' she mouthed, making sure the singer wasn't looking at them.

He nodded. 'He always takes a while to get used to things. Nothing we can do about it. I had kind of hoped he'd be a bit faster than this though ...'

'I'm sure you'll be just fine on Friday.'

'We'll see. Okay, here goes.'

They began the rehearsal, and although it went better than the previous Tuesday session, Jesse still wasn't very happy by the time they finished. Scott had only learned the words to two of the new songs and refused to do any more.

'No way, man. I'll only mess up. Let's stick to what we know.'

Jesse kept shooting glances in Rain's direction and caught her staring at him a couple of times. He knew he shouldn't have encouraged her to come today, but he'd wanted to see her without having to worry about Amber throwing a fit and this seemed the only way.

The jamming session at an end, Scott left and the others headed for home as well. Jesse and Rain were the last ones to leave and when they were alone on the drive, next to his car, she said soothingly, 'You guys were great. I'm looking forward to the concert.'

Jesse sighed. 'No, we weren't. It's so frustrating, because we could be a lot better. Mick and Zane have learned all the new stuff without any problems, but Scott just won't even try. Man, he's being such an asshole! It makes me so pissed off. Instead of wowing the audience, we're just going to sound like some lame karaoke outfit, rehashing other people's songs. Anyone can do that.' He pushed his fingers through his hair, wanting to tear at it instead.

Rain put a hand on his arm. 'One step at a time. You've only had a week, maybe you just need to let Scott adjust more slowly? Not everyone is a natural, you know. He has a good voice.'

'Yeah, I guess you're right. Well, I'd better let you get home. You must be starving, I know I am.' His stomach growled loudly to emphasise this point, which made them both laugh.

'What are you having for dinner?' Rain asked.

'Huh? I don't know. A microwave meal I guess.'

'Want to come and eat with us instead? I mean ...' She looked for a moment as if she regretted the invitation, but then her mouth tightened in determination. 'My mum always makes way too much and she loves having guests.'

'Oh, er ... no, thanks, I don't think so. I, uhm ... other people's parents don't usually like having me over.'

Rain stared at him. 'What do you mean? Why ever not? Do you eat with your fingers or something? Burp at the table?'

'Not exactly.'

'Then there's no problem. Come on, just follow me in your car. Trust me, my mum will be thrilled.'

He groaned and muttered, 'Trust *me*, she won't.' But he

seemed to have no option and if he was perfectly honest, he'd put up with another uncomfortable meal just to spend some more time with her. *Hell, I need to have my head examined.*

'Can you just do me a favour though, please?' Rain sent him a pleading look. 'Pretend like we've both been at Dakota's house studying for exams. That's what I told my parents I'd be doing today.'

'Sure, whatever.' It was no skin off his nose and he doubted her parents would ask him anyway. Jesse looked round. 'Where's your car?'

Her face turned slightly pink, but then she hid behind her hair and muttered something about wanting exercise. 'I've got my bike and I'll try and cycle fast.'

'Forget that, let's just put it in the back seat. I'll pull the top down.'

As the Mustang was a convertible, it wasn't a problem, and although it was really too cold to ride in an open-top car, at least it wasn't raining. 'It'll be fine,' he said when she started to protest. 'It's not that far.'

It didn't take them long to reach Rain's home and as Jesse parked on the drive outside and looked at the imposing clapboard mansion, he swallowed a sigh. *I shouldn't have come. This is going to be another total disaster.*

'Mum, I brought you a guest for dinner,' Rain shouted the minute they walked through the front door of the Gothic house. Jesse wished that he could suddenly become invisible. Although it wasn't as intimidating as the Lawrence's home, it all seemed impossibly rich and he felt like he definitely didn't belong in such surroundings.

To his surprise, Rain's mother emerged from the back of the house with a huge smile of welcome that looked completely genuine. Rain made the introductions and Jesse detected some tension between them, although it didn't seem to be because of him.

'Mum, this is Jesse Devlin. He was studying with us and no one was cooking for him today, so I thought I'd invite him. You don't mind, do you? Jesse, this is my mother, Lady Mackenzie.'

She was a tiny woman, at least half a head shorter than her daughter and with brown curly hair rather than Rain's straight blonde mane. Their features weren't much alike either. Despite being so small though, she had a very firm handshake. 'How wonderful, I love having guests,' she said, echoing Rain's own words earlier.

'Pleased to meet you, ma'am, er, Mrs ... Lady Mackenzie.' Jesse wasn't sure what he was supposed to call her. He'd never met anyone with a title before. It felt like meeting a queen or something, and she talked with a much stronger accent than Rain too. Kind of like people did in old movies. It sounded stuck-up, although she didn't look like she intended it to be.

In fact, he had to admit she seemed nice, especially when she laughed and said, 'Just call me Rowena, dear boy, much less confusing. Now tell me, do you eat pork chops?'

'Yeah, sure. That would be great.'

'Excellent. Rain, show Jesse where to wash his hands and then you can both come and help me take everything into the dining room. Your father will be here in a minute.'

Jesse did as he'd been told, feeling a bit dazed by the friendly Rowena. He'd been going out with Amber for nearly three months now and her mother had never asked him to call her anything other than Mrs Lawrence. It almost felt sinful to call Rain's mother by her first name, but he didn't want to make her angry either so he supposed he'd better.

They carried what seemed like mountains of food into the dining room and Jesse was glad there was nothing fancy. Pork chops, baked potatoes, corn and fried onions, as well as gravy and butter. *I can handle that.* He was also thrilled to note that the place settings had only one knife and fork next to each plate and a spoon for dessert. *At least I won't be making an ass of myself with the cutlery again,* he thought to himself.

'Hello, who have we here, then?' A tall blond man, who looked very much like Rain, had come into the room and was walking towards Jesse with his hand outstretched. Jesse shook it, while Rain again made the introductions.

'This is Jesse Devlin, he's in some of my classes. Remember, I told you about his car, the blue Mustang? Jesse, this is my dad, Sir Anthony Mackenzie.'

'Pleased to meet you, er … Sir Mackenzie.'

'Please, call me Anthony. I leave all that "sir" nonsense in the boardroom.'

'Right, okay.' Jesse wasn't quite sure if the guy really meant it, but he figured he could always ask Rain later. In the meantime, he'd try to avoid calling him anything at all.

'Mm, this smells heavenly, darling.' Sir Anthony beamed at his wife. 'Shall we?'

They all sat down and Jesse was urged to 'tuck in'. He tried to eat slowly at first, but soon noticed that no one was paying attention to the way he ate, so he relaxed and began to enjoy the food. It really was delicious and reminded him of the way his own mother had cooked for him sometimes.

'This is great,' he said to Rain's mom, meaning it wholeheartedly.

'I'm so glad you like it.' She smiled at him. 'Do help yourself to some more. I can't stand leftovers. But don't forget to leave some room for dessert. Lemon meringue pie. I hope you like that?'

'I like everything,' Jesse assured her.

'Excellent. A boy after my own heart. You must come back again soon. It's lovely to meet some of Rain's friends at last.'

Jesse blinked. She really seemed to mean that, but he wasn't given the time to think about it, because in the next minute Rain and her father dragged him into a discussion about Ford Mustangs.

'Jesse's made some adjustments to his, Dad. You should hear it, it sounds so much more … oh, I don't know, just powerful I guess. A tiger compared to your cat.'

'Really? Would you mind if I took a look after dinner?' Sir Anthony smiled at Jesse in a friendly way. 'Obviously, I won't expect you to tell me your secrets, but I've been trying to find someone who could give mine a bit more oomph. It's just so sluggish.'

'No problem. We can go for a quick drive if you like, and then I could have a look at yours maybe? I mean, if you'd like, of course …' *Shit, what am I doing?* A guy like this wasn't going to take his advice any more than Mr Lawrence had.

But Sir Anthony surprised him. 'That sounds wonderful. Has Rain shown you the rest of my little collection?' Sir Anthony nodded towards the back of the house where Jesse assumed the garage was located. 'I only brought my favourites, but I hear you like Lamborghinis.'

Jesse was amazed Rain would have confessed to her father that she'd let Jesse drive the car. He stared at her across the table, but she just smiled and shrugged. She waited a moment until her mom left the room, presumably to get more food, then added in a whisper, 'I had to tell Dad in case someone saw us. I didn't want to give him any more cause to ground me. Although …' A blush spread over her cheeks as if she'd said too much. This was the first Jesse had heard of her being grounded, but he figured if she didn't want to talk about it, it wasn't any of his business, so he didn't comment.

'Oh, right.' Jesse looked at Rain's father. 'I'm sorry

about the Lambo. I kind of got carried away and persuaded Rain ...'

Sir Anthony waved a hand dismissively. 'It's not a problem, dear boy. If Rain considers you a good enough driver, that's fine by me. I trust her judgement. You do have a licence, I take it?' He shot his daughter a look which Jesse couldn't interpret, but again, he thought it best not to mention it.

'Sure I do,' he said, wondering if that was an English joke or something, but no one said anything more about it.

'And as for that grounding, I think we can forget about that now, don't you, Rain? Enough is enough.'

Her eyes lit up. 'Thank you, Dad!'

Rain's mom came back into the room and there was no more talk about the Lamborghini incident. When dinner was over, Jesse realised that at no point had he felt left out or unwelcome, and everyone had made sure he joined in the conversations. In fact, he'd been almost overwhelmed by Rain's parents' kindness.

'Shall we go for a drive, then?' Sir Anthony asked, smiling in anticipation.

'Let the poor boy digest his food first, darling,' Lady Mackenzie protested. 'I'm sure you can see his car some other time. Honestly, you petrolheads are impossible! How about some coffee, Jesse?'

'No thanks, I don't drink coffee. Keeps me awake all night,' Jesse said. He turned to Sir Anthony. 'And I don't mind driving now. It would be my pleasure.'

'Excellent. Rain, are you coming?'

'Well, duh. Of course I am.'

Jesse let Rain's father drive and quickly discovered that he was an even better driver than his daughter. They went out to the disused airfield again and Sir Anthony shouted with delight as Jesse's Mustang handled the corners to his satisfaction.

'This is brilliant,' he said, when they were on the way back to the house again. 'What on earth have you done to it? Rain is right, mine's a non-starter in comparison.'

Jesse grinned. 'Oh, this and that. Let me get my hands on yours and I'll see what I can do.'

'I'd really appreciate that. You'll have to send me a bill though. Charge me by the hour, okay?'

'No, really, that's not necessary,' Jesse started to protest, but was cut off.

'I insist. I wouldn't have you work for nothing, and as I know only too well, teenagers need endless funds.' He glanced at Rain, who was huddled into the back seat. She punched her father lightly on the shoulder.

'I'm not that expensive, not any more. I'm saving you, like, ten thousand pounds at least just by being here for a term.'

'Hmm, yes, I suppose so. Which means I can afford to employ Jesse to fix my Mustang.'

Jesse had to laugh at this weird reasoning and promised to send a bill. He wasn't sure when he'd have time to actually do the work, since he was so busy at the moment with school, band practice, soccer and the part-time job, but he figured he'd fit it in somehow.

The visit to Sir Anthony's garage almost made him speechless. As Rain turned on the lights, Jesse gasped. He started to wonder if the whole evening was a dream. 'Wow,' he breathed as he took in the 'little collection'. 'This is awesome.'

'Well, I wouldn't go quite that far, but I enjoy it,' Sir Anthony laughed. 'Want to drive any of them?'

'I don't know. It's kind of like being taken to a toy shop at Christmas and told to choose just one thing when you want everything.'

'Let me rephrase the question, then,' Sir Anthony said,

grinning at him. 'Would you like to drive one of them today and come back to try the rest some other time?'

'Yes, please.' Without hesitation, Jesse headed for a dark blue Aston Martin Vanquish. 'This one?'

'Good choice. Rain? Keys please.'

As he lay in bed later that night, Jesse's head spun, but he knew one thing – Rain's parents were seriously nice people and she was extremely lucky to have them.

Chapter Fourteen

The day after their evening of driving with her father, Rain found Jesse lounging next to her locker. Amber was nowhere in sight, but then she figured he'd probably have made sure of that before being seen talking to Rain.

'Hello,' she said, as casually as she could. 'What's up?'

'Nothing. Just wanted to say thank you, I guess.'

'For what?' Rain busied herself putting stuff into her locker so she wouldn't have to look at him. His blue eyes seemed to be even brighter than usual today, almost radiating happiness.

'You know, dinner, the driving, just yesterday.' He shrugged and put his arm along the top of her locker door just like that first time. 'It was great.'

She gave him a quick glance and smiled. 'Me too. Thanks for not minding my parents. They can be a bit much sometimes.'

'Are you kidding? They were great!'

'You think? All that "dear boy" stuff is so old-fashioned. And I'm sorry I didn't explain about the title before we got there. I kind of forget about that most of the time.'

'Not a problem. They didn't seem to mind what I called them. And the rest – forget it. Anyone who lets me drive an Aston Martin can call me whatever the hell they like.'

Rain looked up and found him giving her that lazy smile she liked so much. To distract herself from that, she glanced at his arm and the dragon swirling along it. Without thinking, she blurted out, 'You know, I think I do want one.'

'One what?' His smile had turned to confusion.

'Tattoo.' She nodded towards his arm. 'A dragon.'

'What, like this? Are you sure about that? It would take ages.' His eyes had opened wide now and he put his head to one side as if he couldn't believe what he was hearing.

'Not that big. I mean a little one. A small dragon. Maybe like a baby one? Or at least tiny in size.'

'Oh, right. Well, you'd better talk to Steve, the guy who did mine. Want me to introduce you?'

Rain hesitated. If she said yes, that would mean spending more time with Jesse, and that was starting to become more and more dangerous. But she really did want a tattoo and how else would she get one? *Go and find a tattoo parlour yourself,* a little voice inside her urged, but she ignored it.

'Would you mind?' she asked. 'I mean, you could just tell me where it is and I'll find it myself if you prefer.'

'Nah, you'd have to wait months. Steve's real busy. But he might do one for you if I ask. How about this afternoon? We can go straight after soccer practice.'

'Um, sure, thank you. That would be great. Hang on though, aren't I supposed to be eighteen or is it different here in the States?'

Jesse pushed his fingers through his hair and made a face. 'Yeah, technically, but ... could you maybe forge your mom's signature on a letter to say you have permission? Steve says hardly anyone ever checks and if angry parents come to him later, he can show them the letter and say it wasn't his fault.'

'Yes, I can do that. She'll probably kill me, if she ever finds out, but if I tell her it's legal to get a tattoo at seventeen here, I doubt she'll check.'

'What about your dad?'

'Oh, he won't mind. He's very easy-going, as you probably noticed yesterday. He only gets cross when I do something really stupid, like getting myself expelled.' *And drive his car without a licence.* But she didn't add that.

'Cool! So this afternoon, then? Later.'

Rain had no idea where Amber was and she didn't want to ask, but she assumed Jesse had made sure his girlfriend didn't know he was taking Rain to get a tattoo. He'd barely looked at her since they'd hung out at her locker that morning, so he was obviously being extra careful not to make Amber angry. Rain tried not to think about it. *It's not as if we're on a date or anything. He's just taking me to his friend to ask a favour.*

Steve turned out to be a Hell's Angel, or at least that's what he looked like. Leather trousers, leather waistcoat and black T-shirt with AC/DC emblazoned across the front. He had a huge handlebar moustache and a shaved head. But the minute he smiled in welcome, he didn't look scary any more.

'Jesse, my man! S'up?'

They did that bro fist thing Americans seemed so fond of and Rain stood to one side, feeling a bit awkward while they chatted for a while. Finally, they turned to her.

'So you want a tattoo, little lady? What d'ya have in mind?'

'I'd like a small dragon, please. Here.' She pointed to her right forearm. 'Maybe three inches long?'

'Sure. Have a look round to see if there are any you like. Otherwise I'll have to design one specially for you.' Steve indicated the walls, which were covered in all kinds of patterns.

Rain wandered round, looking at them all until her eye fell on a Chinese type dragon. It was beautiful and swirly and just what she wanted, all in black. 'This one, please,' she said.

'Great choice,' Steve agreed. 'I love that one. I've had a cancellation this afternoon, so do you want to get started right away?'

'Um, yes, sure, that would be great.' Rain swallowed hard. *Am I ready for this?* Perhaps she'd been a little bit hasty in deciding to have a tattoo done this minute? After all, it would be there for life.

'Would you like some numbing cream? It'll take a while to work though, so it's faster without.'

Rain didn't want to be seen as a wuss, so she shook her head. How painful could it be? Jesse had had two whole arms done, after all.

'Okay, so have you got the letter of permission?'

Rain handed over the forged letter. She felt bad about that, but didn't think her mum would ever know. She'd printed it out in the library that afternoon and was pleased with the result. *It's only a year until I'm eighteen anyway, so I would've got one then. Can't make any difference.* She knew that wasn't true though and tried to suppress the guilt she felt.

Jesse stayed with her while Steve sat her in a chair, cleaned her arm with antiseptic or some other sterilising stuff and put a stencil of the dragon pattern on her arm. When Steve got out his tattooing machine, Rain looked away and clenched her other fist, but Jesse must have noticed because she felt him put his hand around it and hold tight. 'It's not so bad,' he said. 'Your little dragon won't take long.'

It did hurt like hell from time to time. It was a bit like having something burning and pulling the skin at the same time, or like very slow scratching. But the pain came and went, with Steve swabbing the area clean every few minutes, and it was bearable, mostly because Rain concentrated on the feeling of Jesse holding her hand. He also kept up a conversation with her about her dad's cars and the band and all kinds of stuff, taking her mind off what Steve was doing. At last, when she thought she would soon have to tell them to stop for a while, he declared, 'There, all done.'

Steve applied some antiseptic cream and covered Rain's arm with clingfilm. 'So it stays clean for a while,' he explained. 'You have to wash it three times a day with warm soapy water and put water-based lotion on it after each time.

Try not to let your clothes touch it and don't put it in salt or chlorinated water for three weeks. Here's a care sheet with instructions in case you forget. Any problems, just call me, okay? Number's on there.'

'Thank you. Thank you very much,' Rain smiled at him and drew in a deep breath of relief. Now it was all done, Rain didn't feel any pain, just a slightly grazed sensation. 'How much do I owe you?' She pulled her wallet out of her pocket, but he shook his head.

'Any friend of Jesse's don't pay, especially for a little one like that. It's on the house.'

Rain looked at Jesse and raised her eyebrows. 'Are you sure? I mean, I'm happy to pay.'

'Nah. This one's on me. Enjoy.'

'Wow, thank you. That's very kind.'

Jesse thanked Steve too and then hustled her out of the tattoo parlour. He grinned and nodded at her arm wrapped in plastic. 'So how are you going to keep that from your parents? I forgot it has to heal without touching anything for a while.'

'I'll just have to wear a loose-fitting long-sleeved T-shirt when they're around. I'd rather not show them until it's healed.'

'Yeah, that's probably a good idea. They're going to go ape, huh?'

'Yep, but let's not talk about that. It was kind of Steve to fit me in straight away.'

'He's a nice guy.'

'Well, yes, but I feel bad about not paying.'

'Don't worry about it. I fix his car for free and I gave it a paint job too. We're quits.'

Rain frowned. 'Technically, that means I owe you instead.'

He grinned at her. 'I'm sure I can think of something you

can do to pay me back.' His wicked blue eyes were dancing. 'But I'll take a rain check for now.'

Rain had a feeling she would regret this, but right now she was just happy to have her tattoo. It wasn't until she got home she realised she'd chosen a dragon motif without even considering anything else.

Because that's what Jesse had.

'So are you going to the dance tonight?' Hayley asked Rain on the Friday afternoon. 'You can come with me and Dakota if you want.'

'I don't know. I might just watch the band play, then go home. Are you coming for that part?'

She very carefully didn't refer to the band as Jesse's, although she knew he was the driving force behind them. She had seen the notices all over the school announcing that Escape From Hell were playing live. She still liked the name, it suited them somehow. Zane had told her Jesse was planning on using the stage name Jesse Devil if the band ever made it big, which made it an even better choice.

'Hell, yeah! Try and stop us. We're fans, remember?' Hayley grinned.

'Oh, yes, how could I forget? Just don't throw your knickers at Mick, please!'

'My what?'

'Your underwear.'

Hayley made a face. 'Gross! No way. Anyway, we'll see you there. Unless you want someone to arrive with?'

'No, don't worry, I'll be fine. I'll meet you inside.'

Rain still wasn't convinced she should go, because she had a feeling Jesse might mention her name after all, even though she'd asked him not to. In the end, she decided to get ready, then make a decision later.

For once, there was no soccer practice, so she went home

and had a shower and washed her hair, then applied a lot more make-up than she usually would. She put lashings of mascara, some eyeliner and a bit of dark eye shadow, as well as some blusher to make her high cheekbones appear even more pronounced. A bit of lip gloss finished things off nicely and she was quite pleased with the result until she realised that the look she'd gone for was very 'rock chick'. She almost groaned.

It was how a girlfriend of Jesse's ought to look tonight, but she was nothing to do with him. She sighed and wondered if she should start over, then decided to leave it anyway. If anyone asked, she'd say she'd done it for Zane, who was after all also in the band and now her friend.

'Okay, I might as well go the whole hog,' she muttered, and rooted around in her wardrobe. She came up with a black leather miniskirt, complete with a pattern of dangling chains, a black low-cut strappy top that also showed off her toned stomach, and a sparkly black jacket. High-heeled, bright pink suede ankle boots and black leggings with a swirly pattern completed her outfit. And the dragon tattoo was the icing on the cake. She almost laughed when she caught sight of herself in the mirror. *Definitely rock chick clothes.*

Well, it was too late to change now.

Chapter Fifteen

'Where the hell is he? He should have been here by now.'

Jesse was pacing around backstage, which was really the boy's changing room at Northbrooke High. A makeshift stage had been set up for them at one end of the gym, with all their equipment ready and waiting and some special lighting rigged up by the techie-savvy guys in their class. Everything was go except for Scott.

He hadn't turned up.

'I told him to be here early,' Mick grumbled. 'Stupid jerk. He's probably still sulking about you making him learn those new songs, Jesse.'

'For Christ's sake, I thought we all wanted the same thing – to be signed by a record label. How are we ever going to achieve that if we don't write our own material? No one's going to take on a band that can only play other people's old stuff.'

He pushed his fingers through his hair for the umpteenth time, not caring that it made it stand up even more than usual. He had gelled it a lot so it would be perfect in the spotlights and they'd all put on black eyeliner – 'guyliner', Amber called it – so they'd stand out on stage, but now it probably wouldn't matter. If Scott didn't turn up soon, they were screwed.

At last, their lead vocalist ambled in, but it soon became clear that he wasn't in any state to sing. He was so drunk he could barely stand up.

Jesse swore a blue streak, kicked at the nearest chair and stormed out into the fresh air. He was so angry, he didn't know what to do with himself, but he knew if he stayed inside he'd beat the shit out of Scott. It wouldn't help, but it sure as hell would make him feel better.

Zane came after him. 'Wait up, Jesse. We've still got fifteen minutes to go. Maybe we can pour some coffee into him, sober him up a bit. I can drag him into the shower, make it real cold.'

'Forget it. There's no way you'll get him fit to sing in fifteen minutes.'

'We're a rock band, we can delay a bit, right? It's what the pros always do. Keep the audience waiting, get them excited.'

'No! We're going to have to tell them the gig's off. Damn him!'

He turned a corner of the building and almost collided with a dark shape who muttered, 'Sorry.'

'Rain?' He wasn't sure it was her at first, since she didn't look like she normally did, but there was no mistaking that hair. It slithered around her shoulders, shimmering in the light from the moon. 'What are you doing skulking back here?' The words came out as if he was accusing her of some crime, but he was still too angry to care how he sounded.

'Er, I was just going inside. I ... uhm, hadn't quite made up my mind yet.'

'Why the hell not?' He frowned at her, not understanding, then he remembered that it didn't matter. 'Actually, you might as well go home, because there won't be a gig. Scott is too drunk to sing. It's all off.'

'What? No! Why?'

He shrugged and it was Zane who explained Mick's theory about Scott sulking. 'And his older brother buys him booze by the gallon. He's a real bonehead.'

'That's ridiculous,' Rain said. 'Sulking? How old is he, ten? Well, that does it – you should find someone else to be your lead singer, if you ask me.'

'Yeah, well we would, you know, like, if we had the time, but obviously fifteen minutes, no, ...' Jesse glanced at his watch, 'ten now, actually, isn't really enough. Unless you're offering to do it yourself?' He knew he was being horrible and sarcastic, taking his anger out on her, but he just couldn't help it. He was so disappointed because he'd really thought they would be great tonight.

He saw her take a deep breath. 'Okay, then, I will,' she said, lifting her chin a notch.

Jesse stared at her, his mouth falling open. 'What did you say?'

'I'll do it. I know all the songs just as well as Scott. I was listening when you jammed, remember? And I wrote the words, so I'm not likely to forget those. We'll have to do more than two of the new ones though. I'm not so good on the old stuff.'

Jesse swallowed hard and kept staring at her. 'Are you serious?'

Zane joined in. 'Yeah, you sure? There will be a lot of people watching. I mean, I'm not trying to scare you or anything, but ...'

Rain smiled. 'Don't worry about that. I was in the choir at my old school and I often had to sing solo. There were loads of parents and people watching. Doesn't bother me. I like being in the limelight. I'm not sure if my voice is right for your kind of music, though, so you're both going to have to sing with me. Maybe together we'll be okay?'

'Sure, whatever you say.' Jesse beamed at her, hardly able to believe his luck.

'Sweet!' Zane grinned like an idiot and slapped her on the back.

Jesse felt the knot in his stomach dissolve and his shoulders relax. So great was the relief, he reached out and hugged her tight. Too tight, judging by the muffled squeak of protest that came from somewhere near his shoulder.

'Let the poor girl breathe and don't break her ribs,' Zane laughed, 'or she definitely won't be able to sing. Anyway, what are we hanging around out here for? We've got a show to do. Get your asses inside, people. Let's decide the order of the songs.'

Jesse laughed and grabbed Rain's hand, pulling her along. When they came into the changing room, he noticed for the first time what she was wearing and he smiled and gave her the thumbs up. 'Perfect,' he said, and almost laughed again as she blushed. 'You sure you're not going to be embarrassed out there?' he asked, but somehow he knew he was the one that caused her to go red, no one else. That thought made him feel even happier.

Mick was sitting with a practically comatose Scott, looking despondent, but he cheered up instantly when told what was happening. 'Atta girl.' He smiled at Rain.

'Okay, you need to do some vocal exercises or something?' Jesse asked her.

'Maybe a few. Hold on. Can you accompany me on the guitar, I'll just sing the first verse of "Temptation".'

'No problem.'

When she started to sing, Jesse knew they were going to be alright. More than alright.

They were going to be absolutely freaking fantastic.

Rain had never suffered from stage fright, in fact, like she'd said, she used to revel in the attention, so she wasn't worried about performing. She *was* a bit anxious about letting Jesse down, in case she didn't live up to his expectations. But in the end she reasoned that she had to be better than nothing, which is what he'd had before.

There was a last-minute hitch when Amber walked into the makeshift changing room and did a double take at the sight of Rain. 'What's she doing in here?' she hissed. 'Get her out, now. You promised, Jesse.' Amber no longer had a bandage on her nose, but even with carefully applied make-up, you could tell she still had a black eye. Rain knew being hit on the nose often had that effect and the bruising lingered, but although she regretted hitting the girl, she still felt Amber had deserved it. Clearly Amber wasn't in a forgiving mood though.

Jesse seemed to know just how to handle her, however, because he went over to talk to her and soon had her calmed down. Rain heard snatches of their conversation, and although his words annoyed her a bit since half of what he said wasn't true, she knew they didn't have time for Amber's histrionics right now. The gig was more important.

'She came with Zane … Scott drunk … persuaded her to do it … you know how important this is to me …' Jesse was gesticulating at the now snoring Scott and had turned Amber away so she wasn't facing Rain. His persuasive powers worked and soon she was putty in his hands.

'Okay, sweetie. Go show them out there. I'll be cheering for you.' Amber stood on tiptoe to give him a kiss, but he turned his head so she could only reach his cheek. Rain looked away and concentrated on the lyrics she was running through inside her head.

She'd show them alright. Amber most of all.

The crowd in the gym were now shouting, clapping and stamping their feet and Dr A came into the room to tell them it was time.

'Okay, let's go,' Jesse said, and they ran out onto the stage.

Rain was glad she'd dressed the way she had. It made her feel like she belonged up there. She got a huge thrill from the roar that went up as the guys picked up their instruments and she grabbed the microphone. It was already turned on, Dr A had whispered to her, so all she had to do was wait for Jesse to play the introductory chords on his guitar, with Mick picking up the beat and Zane joining in on bass. The time had come to show what they could do.

Jesse had decided they should start with 'Temptation', since that was the one they knew best and Rain was happy with that. The music turned out to be well suited to her voice, which was deep and dark for a girl, but very strong. As she began to sing the first few lines, she looked over at Jesse and caught his look of utter joy and encouragement. The grin he gave her warmed her all the way down to her toes and he and Zane joined her in the chorus.

The crowd liked it too and were soon clapping along and whistling their approval. She'd been right in thinking it was a catchy song. They erupted into cheering and foot-stamping when it came to an end and only stopped when Jesse struck the chords for the next one. The band got into their stride and continued with song after song, only stopping for brief pauses so Rain could have a drink of water. In the end, they played three of the songs she and Jesse had written, including 'Dark Side' which went down really well with their audience. Then they continued with covers of well-known rock anthems and finally Avenged Sevenfold's 'Dear God' – one of Rain's absolute favourite power ballads – as an encore, because the crowd demanded more than they had.

They accepted the applause together at the front of the stage, the four of them holding hands and bowing in unison like actors in a play. Then the three guys stepped back and made Rain take a bow on her own, which embarrassed her because she knew the others had contributed just as much. Dr A jumped up onto the stage and shouted, 'Escape From Hell, everybody! Let's hear it for our own budding superstars!'

Rain laughed. She couldn't imagine the staid old headmaster of Blakeborough ever acting like that, let alone saying a name like Escape From Hell with a straight face, but here it felt right. They got off the stage and back into the changing room, where Rain sank onto the nearest bench. She was completely exhausted.

'Rain, Rain, you were amazing!' Dakota and Hayley had pushed their way in and crowded round her, jumping up and down.

She grinned at them. 'You think? Thank you. I didn't see you guys in the crowd, but then I didn't dare look at anyone in particular, in case it made me forget the lyrics.'

'We were right at the front to one side, but no worries – of course you didn't have time to stare at us! But why didn't you tell us you were going to sing? We didn't have a clue.'

'Me neither.' Rain laughed. 'It was kind of a last minute thing.'

'You're kidding. You guys sounded like you'd played together all your lives. Absolutely freaking awesome.'

'Thanks, I'm glad it went okay.'

'More than okay. And we're loving the tattoo – so cool! When did you get it done?'

'Oh, just the other day. It's not really healed yet.'

'Well, it looks great. See you outside, right? Don't you dare go home now, or we'll come and drag you back,' Dakota threatened.

'All right, I'll stay. For a while.'

Jesse and the others had been busy accepting congratulations too, but finally everyone left them alone to wind down and catch their breath. Even Amber had been persuaded to go and wait outside in the gym, where the DJ for the dance now started everyone off with the latest dance track.

Jesse came over and sat down next to Rain, leaning his head against the wall the same way she was doing. He closed his eyes and so did she, totally drained from the performance. When she opened them again after a while, they were the only two people left in the locker room.

'I seem to keep having to thank you,' Jesse said, turning to look at her. 'I can't tell you how awesome you were out there. Seriously, I almost dropped my guitar. I had no idea you could sing like that. You sounded and looked like a pro.'

'Thanks, but it was all down to you for writing such great music. It just happened to suit my voice.'

'Bullshit! You're being too modest. Will you sing with us again? Join the band? Please? I think we can really go places and as a song-writing team, we're pretty damn good too, even if I say it myself.'

She hesitated, then shook her head. 'No, Jesse. Thanks, but no thanks. I'm going back to England soon. My dad's found a place for me for next term.'

That was totally untrue, but it didn't matter. She saw him frown and steeled herself to lie some more if she had to. Out there on the stage earlier she had allowed herself to dream about how great they could be together, and she had finally acknowledged that she'd fallen for him. She didn't just have a crush on him, the way she'd had with Milo, she was head over heels in love and there wasn't a thing she could do about it. But he was with Amber and no matter how good the chemistry was between Rain and Jesse when they performed, she couldn't stand the thought of being with him every day and yet having to watch him go off with Amber afterwards. It would be too painful. Much better to make a clean break now.

'He must be one hell of a guy, your boyfriend, since you're so keen to get back,' Jesse said harshly, his eyes clearly showing his disappointment at her refusal.

'What, Milo?' Rain answered without thinking. 'I'm not going back to that slimebag. It's his fault I'm here – he blamed the whole tequila incident on me because he's shit-scared of his dad and since he'd never been caught playing pranks before and I had, I was the one who went down. All my so-called friends backed him up. No doubt he bribed them.' Rain snorted. 'I wouldn't go back to him if he was the last guy on earth.'

'So what's the problem, then? Why can't you stay here?' Jesse stood up and faced her. He looked like he wanted to shake her, but was holding back, his emotions on a tight rein. Rain closed her eyes so that he wouldn't see the truth in them.

'I don't belong here,' she said, the words coming out in a harsh whisper.

'You're wrong,' he said. 'But have it your way,' he added bitterly. 'We're obviously not good enough for the likes of you, Ice Girl. Well, maybe this will make you think of us sometimes and wonder if you made the right choice.'

She found herself hauled to her feet, slamming into his chest, and before she had time to react, he was kissing her fiercely, hungrily, almost as if trying to punish her. Her eyes opened wide and she saw the anger in his gaze, but also something else – something which burned her and set her veins on fire instantly. With a half-strangled sob, she threw her arms around his neck and kissed him back.

He crushed her to him and she could barely breathe, but it didn't matter. She was where she wanted to be and she wanted him even closer. Tangling her fingers in his hair, she opened her mouth to his kisses. She'd been kissed before, but it had never felt like this, the passion inside her erupting like a furnace. He tasted so good, felt wonderful to hold and for the moment he was all hers.

The kiss seemed to go on forever, but at the same time, it was over too quickly. As soon as it came to an end they pulled apart, staring at each other, breathing heavily. There was confusion in his eyes, probably echoed in hers, she thought, but she realised immediately that this kiss didn't change anything. He hadn't meant anything by it, other than to punish her for not doing what he wanted. She felt a sudden urge to lash out at him and hurt him the way he was hurting her, and somehow she found her voice first.

'Maybe you're the one who will remember what you've lost instead,' she said mockingly, and turned on her heel to march off towards the gym.

She wanted nothing more than to run home and cry until she'd run out of tears, but she was also angrier than she'd ever been in her life. She would show him that the kiss had meant nothing to her either. He could go back to his stupid girlfriend and rot in hell. She was going to forget him and have fun.

Chapter Sixteen

Jesse stared after her and tried to make sense of what had just happened. He had intended to make her change her mind, show her what she'd be missing if she went back to England. Instead he was the one who ended up feeling as if he'd lost everything. He sank down onto the bench again and buried his head in his hands. Nothing made sense any more.

He was still on a high from the rapturous applause they'd received, but at the same time he wanted to punch something out of sheer frustration. He wanted Rain in the band, it was as simple as that. Without her, they were nothing, complete losers. What was the matter with the girl? Why couldn't she see how great a team they made? Sure, the songs were good, but it had been her singing that really made them stand out. Scott could never do them justice, he could see that now.

He felt his dreams come crashing down around him. For a while there, on the stage, he'd been so sure it was all coming together at last – the band, the music, the fame that would spread. A recording deal seemed within his grasp and that was his ticket out of here, his own escape from hell. He would never have to see his dad again.

But now it was slipping away, like water through a sieve. And it was all Rain's fault. *Damn her!*

With a sigh he stood up. There was nothing he could do about it now. He'd probably done enough damage already with that stupid kiss. No, *kisses*, plural, his brain amended, but he didn't want to think about those because if he did he might just go crazy. He headed out into the gym and went in search of Amber and his other friends. There was no need to tell anyone just yet. For this one evening, at least, he would bask in the glory and pretend everything was right with the world. Tomorrow was another day.

Amber clung to him like a leech, screeching at him the moment she caught sight of him. 'Wow, my rock god!' He winced, but put his arms around her anyway. She was soft and she smelled good – although not as good as Rain had, but he wouldn't think about that – and she seemed willing to let him do just about anything. She even let him hold her butt when they danced, something she normally hated. Jesse made the most of it.

Every time they stopped to talk to someone, she preened as if the fact that he'd been a success was somehow partly down to her.

'I always knew he could do it,' she said, over and over again, her voice breathless, excited. 'He's worked so hard, he deserves to be successful.'

That annoyed him. *What the hell does she know about it?* She'd never even wanted to listen to any of his songs before. But he didn't say anything. What was the point? He hated picking fights; he'd had enough of that kind of thing in his life. All he wanted was some peace and quiet, and to be happy.

'Let's dance some more,' Amber urged, and he joined her on the dance floor. He wasn't a great dancer, but he didn't make a total ass of himself either, like some people. Out of the corner of his eye he saw Rain dancing first with Zane, then Mick, then Cody Knight of all people. She danced gracefully, her moves understated, yet very sexy. A part of him wished he could dance with her too, but he knew he never would now.

A slow dance started up and the lights dimmed. Unconsciously, he steered Amber closer to where Rain was attempting to keep Cody's wandering hands in check. Jesse's gaze met hers over the shoulders of their respective partners and for a moment they stared at each other. He felt almost as if some kind of current was passing between them, but she broke it off by turning away. He saw her pull Cody closer and the two of them laughed at something. Jesse felt as if someone had twisted a knife inside him and insight flashed through his brain.

He was in love with Rain. Had been from the moment he saw her. *Oh, hell, no!*

Without thinking, he twirled off in another direction, anywhere except where he could see her. He didn't want to be in love with her, didn't want to be in love with anyone. It was too painful. He'd loved his mom, but she had died and left him behind with that bastard, his dad. Now Rain was leaving too and he couldn't bear it. It was all too much.

Gritting his teeth, he pulled Amber close for a slow kiss, hoping to erase the memory of that other kiss somehow, anyhow. But he knew he didn't have a hope in hell. Nothing would ever compare.

'Jesse? Hey, what's the matter with you, man?'

'What?' Jesse was sitting on a cold bench outside school, smoking a joint he'd bought off one of the stoners. He hated the things normally and hadn't smoked one in years, not since experimenting with such things in junior high, and he felt very strange. At least he was calm now, even if he was having trouble focusing on Zane.

'Are you high?' Zane sat down next to him and took the joint away, sniffing it suspiciously. 'I thought you stopped doing this ages ago? You said we weren't going to go down that road if we became famous. That's just stupid.'

'Yeah, I did.' Jesse grabbed it back anyway.

'So why are you smoking one now? You should be dancing around, celebrating our success, not sitting here by yourself getting all mellow.'

'Nothing to celebrate,' Jesse said. 'Rain said no.'

'No to what? You're not making sense, man,' Zane complained.

'She won't sing with us. Won't be in the band. We're nothing without her, nothing. I need her.'

'*You* need her? You mean, *we* need her, right? Or are we talking about something else here?'

Jesse stared at the ground. He didn't want to look at Zane because he knew his friend usually saw way too much and he just couldn't discuss this with him or anyone. It was too painful.

'Look, maybe I can talk her round,' Zane said after a while. 'She listens to me. Well, sometimes anyway.'

Jesse shook his head. 'No, too late. She's got a place at some stuck-up school in England next semester. She's leaving.'

'Next semester? Then we have a whole month or more to persuade her to change her mind. Come on, think positive. We'll make her see what she'd be missing.'

Jesse laughed harshly. 'Already tried that. Made a complete ass of myself. She probably hates me now and I deserve it.'

Zane frowned. 'What the hell did you do? Jump her?'

'Something like that,' Jesse muttered.

'For Christ's sake, what's got into you?' Jesse didn't answer so Zane shook his shoulder. 'Jesse, what's going on? Talk to me, or I can't help you.'

'No one can help me. Just go away, Zane. Leave me alone. I want to be mellow in peace.'

'With that?' Zane pointed at the joint.

Jesse stared at it and couldn't remember why he'd thought it was a good idea to smoke one. He threw it onto the ground in disgust. Zane was right. It wasn't helping and he'd sworn never to do stuff like that again. *I'll never become famous that way*. He stomped on it with his heel and pushed it into the dirt. *Not that there's any chance of that now anyway …*

'That's more like it,' Zane commented. 'Now get a grip, man. I'll talk to you later. And I'll make you give me some answers tomorrow when you're normal again.'

'Yeah, whatever.'

Zane walked off and Jesse watched him. It looked like he was moving in slow motion and it seemed funny so he laughed. Then he remembered that he wasn't going to laugh ever again. There was nothing to laugh at.

Life was shit.

'Rain? Rain, are you listening to me?'

'Huh? Sorry, Zane, what were you saying?' Rain tried to concentrate on her surroundings, but it was an effort and somehow it was easier just to shut everything out. Zane wasn't one to give up though, so she figured she'd better pay attention for a little while at least.

'I said, are you okay? You look like you haven't slept for weeks.'

'Thanks. You really know how to make a girl feel good about herself.' She gave him a small smile to show that she hadn't really taken offence.

'You know what I mean. Listen, if it was something Jesse said or did, then I'm sure he didn't mean it …'

'Jesse has nothing to do with anything,' Rain said more firmly than she'd intended, glaring at Zane. 'Please don't talk to me about him, okay? I do *not* want to be in your stupid band, so if he's sent you to try and persuade me, you can forget it. Got that?'

Zane held up his hands in self-defence. 'Whoa, take it easy, don't bite my head off. I wasn't going to say anything about the band. You've made your feelings quite clear on that subject. But I know Jesse's upset you in some way and I think he's hurting about it too, so I'd like to try and mediate here. You know, a little give and take and we could all be friends again.'

She snorted. 'No way. Friends. Hah!'

'What the hell did he do to you?' Zane was looking totally despairing.

'Why don't you ask him that?'

'I have and he won't tell me. Did he … I mean, he didn't hurt you or anything, did he? He's usually not the violent type.'

Rain narrowed her eyes at him. 'Yes, he did. He hurt me more than you can ever imagine, but not physically. It's not something you can fix, so just leave me alone now, okay? I'll still be friends with you, but not if you're going to talk about Jesse all the time.'

'Jeez, I just wish I knew what he'd said …'

'*Zane.*'

'Okay, okay, I'll shut up already.' He sighed. 'Right, change of subject. Are you coming on the Senior outing next week?'

'Outing?' Rain's mind went blank for a moment, then she remembered. 'Oh, you mean that stupid "Bonding Day" or whatever Dr A called it. Out in the forest? Yeah, I guess I don't have a choice. It's compulsory, isn't it? Any idea what we'll be doing?'

'As a matter of fact, I have. Some of us have contacts in the principal's office.' He grinned.

'Okay, so tell me, then.' Rain wasn't really interested, but it was a better topic of conversation than Jesse.

'Well, first, we're going to do some archery and fake clay pigeon shooting, then we'll be divided into teams to do tug-of-war and then—'

'Tug-of-war? What are we, little kids?' Rain stared at Zane in disbelief.

'No, but it's a bonding exercise, remember? We have to work together. Teamwork.'

'What complete bollocks.'

'"Bollocks"?' He laughed. 'I like that word.'

'Zane,' Rain said warningly. She was so not in the mood to be teased about her British-ness again. 'How is archery or shooting a bonding exercise, then? You do that by yourself.'

He shook his head. 'Nuh-uh. We'll be in teams there too, so the other team members will cheer us on to do well.'

'Fantastic.' Her voice dripped with sarcasm. 'I can't wait … And all this in a freezing cold forest at the beginning of November?'

'Oh, yeah. Well, an activity centre in a freezing cold forest. And last, but not least, after lunch we get to do some orienteering.'

'Wonderful! That will just make my day, I'm sure.' Rain sighed. 'I guess I'd better go to the supermarket and get some supplies beforehand. Sounds like it's going to be a long day. Chocolate will be a must.'

'Will you be on my team?'

'Sure, why not, but only if Dakota and Hayley can too.'

Zane put his head to one side and raised his eyebrows slightly. 'Am I supposed to read something significant into that or are you just bringing them as support?'

Rain thought about that for a while before replying. She was pretty sure that Dakota was seriously crushing on Zane and she figured there was no reason why everyone had to be miserable. If she could do some matchmaking, that might make her feel as if her time in Northbrooke hadn't been a total waste. She smiled mischievously at him. 'Are you sure you want an answer to that?'

He grinned back. 'Yes, as a matter of fact, I'm pretty sure I do.'

'Then maybe you can guess for yourself?'

'Hmm, let me think. It couldn't possibly be that a certain young lady desires my company?'

Rain laughed and realised it was the first time in days she'd felt like laughing. Zane really was good for her. It was a shame she couldn't have fallen in love with him instead. 'You're getting warm,' she said.

'Would her name happen to start with a *D*?'

'Got it in one. And if I'm not totally mistaken, there's one whose name starts with an *H* who's rather fond of Mick, so you might want to get him onto your team too.'

Zane's grin broadened. '"Rather fond", huh? Jolly good.' She had to admit he was getting very good at putting on a British accent, but she knew she couldn't let him get away with teasing her like that. She pushed him hard so he almost toppled off the bench they were sitting on, which only made him chuckle. 'Okay, okay, I meant, aha, I thought so.'

Rain grew serious again. 'Hold on a sec. Maybe I shouldn't have told you this because I know you're never serious about dating and stuff. I don't want anyone to get hurt.'

'Don't worry. I can be serious when I find the right girl, I promise.'

'Okay, just checking. Go and get your team together, then.'

'Yes, ma'am.' He stood up and saluted her, like a soldier, and she pretended to kick him but missed.

'God, you're so annoying, Zane,' she huffed, but she knew that he was the only person who could cheer her up even a little bit at the moment and she was grateful to him for trying.

Chapter Seventeen

Jesse's eighteenth birthday was coming closer and that meant moving out of his dad's house, no matter what. It would have been great if Escape From Hell could have been his ticket out of town, but even without that to look forward to, he was damned if he'd live with the guy a second longer than he had to. He earned enough from his part-time job working with cars to be able to get by until he graduated from high school, provided he could find somewhere cheap to live. He'd have to start asking around.

He wasn't a hoarder, so he didn't have a whole lot of stuff. There were some clothes of course, a few books, posters, CDs and DVDs, plus his guitar and a couple of other things. It wouldn't take him long to pack that up, so there was no point doing it beforehand. That would only give his dad another reason to pick a fight, he was sure.

He remembered there was some of his mom's stuff though, up in a kind of attic area above the hallway. It could only be reached via a folding down ladder, but Jesse figured he might as well have a look. *She was my mom, so I have a right to at least some of her things, right?*

He waited until his dad had gone off to the bar one evening, then opened the ceiling hatch and pulled down the ladder. The opening wasn't huge, so he had some trouble getting through, but he managed it and found a light switch. The storage area was dusty and smelled damp. He made a face. *Damn, what does the old man keep up here?* It looked like a bunch of junk, not even fit to have a garage sale with.

It wasn't possible to stand upright since the ceiling was low, so he crawled on all fours along the planking that constituted the makeshift floor. He rummaged in a couple of boxes and an old suitcase, but this raised so much dust he sneezed.

'What *is* all this shit?'

He found a chest with some old toys in it – his, he assumed, although he only remembered playing with a few of them. They weren't worth taking though, so he abandoned that and crawled further in under the eaves. At last, in a corner, he spotted what he'd been looking for – a box labelled 'LILY'S'.

There was only the one, so Jesse dragged it to the opening and carried it downstairs into his room. He cleaned it with a wet cloth then went to close up the hatch, just in case his dad came home early.

With his door shut and locked, he went through the contents. Some jewellery, two photo albums – both filled with photos of him as a baby and small boy – some books, letters and a few porcelain figurines. *This is the total sum of Mom's life?* Jesse couldn't believe there could be so little. *But then, she never bought stuff to fill the house with. There was no money for unnecessary crap.* And her clothes had probably gone to charity years ago.

Feeling very depressed and lonely, he flicked through the photo albums. *Why did you have to die, Mom? Where the hell were you going?* She'd been on the point of leaving Tom the night the accident happened, he knew that much. Jesse could still hear the argument in his head that had ended with her walking out and driving off too fast.

'I'll be back soon, baby,' she'd whispered to him before she left. 'I know someone who can help us, I've just got to go ask. You wait here, okay?' But not long after, the police had come to tell them she'd smashed into another vehicle and died instantly.

Grief tore through him as images from that evening flashed through his mind, but he suppressed it. His mom had died a long time ago and he was over it. He just wished he had someone he could talk to so he didn't always feel so alone. But he'd always kept his thoughts to himself and there weren't even any relatives left who'd remember Lily.

Jesse glanced at the letters from some girl called Mandy. It was all just girly gossip and filled with exclamation marks and capital letters for words like 'love' and 'kiss' and 'the one'. Jesse shook his head. *I don't want any of this, except maybe the photos.* At least a few of them had his mom in them too, looking like he remembered her. He put them to one side.

And maybe the jewellery? He looked in the velvet pouch which contained a couple of rings, some earrings and a silver cross on a chain. That was kind of cool, so he decided to wear that. The rest, he'd just keep.

As he was putting the other stuff back into the box, something fluttered out of one of the books. It was another letter, but it had "Addressee unknown" stamped all over it. Jesse tried to make out the name of the person it was addressed to and when he did, he froze.

R. Linden, c/o Altavista Music Company, Miami, Florida.

Jesse blinked and stared at the envelope again and muttered, '*What the f...!?*'

With suddenly shaking fingers, he pulled out the letter inside and scanned it.

Dear Rick,

I know you probably get letters like this every day from crazy fans, but this is the honest truth so please don't throw this away unread!

Even though you might not believe me, I just wanted

to write and tell you that you have a son. I swear I'm not making this up and I'm pretty sure you'll remember me, since we spent a whole weekend together (and we did talk on the phone a couple times too, although I know you were so busy you didn't have time to come back to Northbrooke). I enclose a photo of me with our baby boy and hope you like it?

He's called Jesse and he has an official dad because I had to get married when I couldn't get hold of you to let you know. I kind of figured you weren't the marrying type anyhow, and Jesse will need a man to help him grow up.

If you get this and you want to come see him, please write to me pretending you're one of my girlfriends and we can arrange to meet. I'm sure you'll agree he is just gorgeous. In fact, he looks a lot like you!

That's all I guess. I'm not asking anything from you except maybe some of your time and for you to meet your son. I hope you will come.

Love always, Your Lily

Jesse felt completely numb and the words on the page danced in front of his eyes for a moment. *Rick Linden?* The *Rick Linden of* Snake? *No fucking way!*

He remembered Rain's teasing remark the first day they met about how he looked like the famous rocker. *But that was just a joke!* Except ... it would seem it wasn't.

It was like someone had hit him real hard, right in the gut, knocking all the air out of his lungs, making him want to keel over. He struggled to take in the simple fact stated in the letter. 'This can't be true,' he muttered, and read it one more time. But it looked like his mom had spent some time with Rick, maybe when he was playing some concerts nearby, and she'd obviously slept with him. A fan girl. A groupie.

My mom! The thought almost made him laugh hysterically, but it wasn't funny at all and it was pretty clear she'd been in love, even if Rick Linden hadn't.

'*He has an official dad.*' The sentence reverberated through his skull and he said the conclusion out loud: 'Tom Devlin isn't my dad.'

The words, even whispered, sounded heavy and final somehow.

Tom Devlin is not *my dad!* But why the hell would the guy marry a woman who was pregnant with some other man's child?

Had Tom been totally in love with Lily and not cared? Or did she not tell him? It was pretty clear to Jesse that Tom must have found out at some point. *That's why he's been so hard on me.*

Strangely that made him feel better. The guy actually had a reason. And he wasn't beating up on his own flesh and blood.

'Why didn't he ever tell me?' Jesse couldn't figure that out.

But Tom wasn't his dad. That was the only thing that was important now. Suddenly, Jesse was filled with relief so great he let out a huge breath he didn't know he'd been holding onto. Relief that he was free to go his own way. Relief that he didn't have to feel guilty about not loving Tom as a son should love his father. He would confront Tom when he felt ready, but not before. For now, he would keep this to himself until he could get his head around it.

That was going to be tough.

Rick Linden? Who would even believe me?

Chapter Eighteen

The 'Bonding Day' had been Dr A's brainchild and he was nauseatingly enthusiastic about the whole thing, to the point where Jesse thought he might want to throw up. It was a simple trip to the forest, as far as he was concerned, and it would probably be boring as hell.

To his surprise, Amber and her friends had been planning for it for days. 'We've got to make sure we have the right gear, honey,' she'd told him, but he wasn't really interested in what she meant so didn't ask her to explain.

He knew it was going to be cold – it was early November after all – and even though it hadn't snowed yet, the temperature had been dropping recently. So he put on thermal underwear, two pairs of warm socks, hiking boots, a huge waterproof jacket with several sweaters underneath, and a hat, scarf and gloves. He also brought a rucksack with a big lunch, a packet of Oreo cookies and several bottles of water, plus a Swiss Army knife and some matches. Who knew what they'd be asked to do, and he figured these might come in handy.

When he caught sight of Amber and her friends, however, he finally understood what she'd meant. They were all dressed in new outfits, similar, but not exactly alike, which consisted of brand new hiking boots in flashy colours – Amber's were bright pink – skintight jeans and short bomber jackets. Instead of hats they wore little fluffy ear muffs and their scarves were those flimsy type things made of printed silk that looked pretty but didn't actually do anything to keep you warm. Amber's had 'Gucci' printed all along the edge. Jesse frowned.

'Amber, are you sure it's a good idea to go out in brand

new hiking boots? They're going to give you blisters. You'd be better off with something comfortable.'

'Oh, come on, Jesse, we won't be going that far. They're taking us there by bus. Don't you like them? I thought they were just darling.' She held out a dainty foot for him to inspect and he had to agree they were sweet. A bit too sweet for his liking though. *Pink, for God's sake!*

'Sure, very nice.' They would have looked better on a five-year-old, but he kept that thought to himself.

There were a couple of coaches waiting in the parking lot outside school, and soon everyone was on board and they set off. After a forty-five-minute journey, they turned onto some smaller tracks and finally arrived at their destination, an activity centre out in the forest.

'This should be fun,' Amber said as they filed out of the bus. 'I'm good at archery.'

'You are?' Jesse was surprised.

'Yeah, we did it for gym a couple of years ago. I was best in the class. The teacher said I had great technique.'

'Well, good.'

Dr A clapped his hands. 'Okay, listen up people. I want you all to divide into teams of eight. If there's anyone left over at the end, I'll assign them to a team, but try to include everyone. Come on, hustle.'

Jesse saw Zane and Mick standing with Dakota and Hayley, and before Amber could protest, he grabbed her hand and steered her in Zane's direction. 'Come on, let's be with my friends for a change,' he said. 'I am so not spending a whole day with Cody and Co.' He'd been listening to Cody on the bus, bragging about how he was going to beat everyone at shooting and archery, and he couldn't stand to be around the guy another second.

'But Jesse, I want to be with Becky,' Amber protested. 'We made sure our outfits matched.'

'For Christ's sake, this isn't a fashion parade,' Jesse muttered. 'But bring her, if you want.'

'No, she wants to be with Max Davison. She's still hoping … Well, anyway, but can we at least sit with them when we eat?'

'Yeah, whatever.'

Too late, Jesse realised that Rain was also part of Zane's group. She had been standing behind the others, and by the time he caught sight of her, he'd already asked Zane if he could join his team.

'Sure, no problem. Now we just need one more person,' Zane said. 'How about Scott?' He shouted over to their former band member, but he'd been sulking ever since the night of the concert and shook his head now. Before they had time to find someone else, Cody materialised next to their group. 'I'll be in your team. You could so do with a great archer, right?'

'Err …' Zane stared at Cody, then back at Jesse with his eyebrows raised.

Cody sidled up to Rain and put an arm round her shoulders. 'You'd appreciate a real man on your team, wouldn't you? I can show you the best way of holding a shotgun. Wouldn't want you ladies to be scared.' He gave her what he obviously considered an irresistible smile, but Rain looked less than impressed.

She went all stiff and glared at him while shrugging his arm off. 'Thanks, Cody, but I'm pretty sure I can figure it out for myself. And the only scary thing around here is you.'

'Aw, come on. Lighten up, Blondie!'

'Don't call me that, Jock Boy.'

Jesse was just about to suggest Cody might be better off on another team when Dr A shouted, 'Get a move on!' and the moment to protest was lost. Jesse stared at Zane in dismay and they made a face at each other behind Cody's back, but all the other teams looked full now so there was nothing they could do.

'Bugger,' Zane whispered when Cody moved out of earshot and tried to charm Dakota instead. Zane threw a teasing grin at Rain, who hit him on the arm.

'What?' Jesse looked from one to the other, but Rain wouldn't meet his eyes.

'Don't worry about it. It's a British thing.' Zane chuckled.

Jesse just nodded. *Whatever.* They were obviously great buddies now and although it pissed him off, he knew Zane was just being his usual friendly self and probably didn't mean anything by it. As for Rain, he didn't know what to think.

As they set off towards the cordoned off area where they were going to do laser clay pigeon shooting, Jesse glanced briefly in Rain's direction. She hadn't dressed up for the occasion, quite the opposite, and he was impressed by her practicality.

A huge padded jacket with a hood edged with fake fur covered her from neck to just above the knees. Underneath she seemed to have several fleeces, a normal scarf and combat trousers. No tight jeans or pink hiking boots for her, just a pair of sensible old worn ones, and crammed onto her head was a knitted hat. She, too, carried a small backpack and Jesse wondered what she had in it. Hopefully not chicken salad, which was what he suspected Amber had brought in her minuscule pink Hermes bag.

Man, he was really starting to hate chicken salad.

Rain seemed very quiet and withdrawn and didn't look at him. She didn't really talk much to anyone and it made Jesse feel bad since it was his fault. He wondered if he should try to apologise, but for what? *For wanting her to stay? For kissing her?* He wasn't sorry for either of those things, even though he probably should be. He looked down at Amber, who was hanging onto his arm as if she'd never let go. She was the person he should really apologise to. He knew he should have finished with her the second he realised he was in love with someone else, but if Rain was leaving, there didn't seem any point.

He sighed. *Why is everything so complicated?*

They were assigned an instructor for the shooting. 'Okay, everyone, listen up while I explain. Laser clay pigeon shooting is almost like the real thing, but very safe. Anyone can do it, even little kids.' He held up a shotgun. 'This here gun's been modified and instead of firing real shots, it sends out infrared beams.' He pointed towards the far end of the lawn they were standing on, where a man sat next to some kind of machine. 'That thing over there is called a trap and it will shoot real clay targets up into the air at great speed. They look kind of like mini UFOs but they're usually called birds. Any questions so far?'

They all shook their heads.

'Great. Now when you guys shoot at the targets, if you hit one with your beam it will send a signal back to our computers.' This time he pointed towards a little tent to one side behind him. 'When you fire, you'll hear a sound like a shotgun, but it's fake so don't be scared. And if you hit the target, you'll get a satisfying noise like breaking clay.'

He demonstrated how to hold it, with the shotgun tucked into his shoulder. 'It doesn't kickback like a real gun so it's completely safe, as I said. Anyone here know how to shoot already?' he asked, and Rain put up a hand.

'I shoot with my dad in England,' she muttered when Zane raised an eyebrow at this.

'Good, then you can have first go,' the man said. He gave Rain the shotgun while he told her where the bird was likely to be and the best place to shoot it, then she raised it to her shoulder. 'Ready? Okay, here goes.'

Two fluorescent orange coloured discs flew up into the air and Rain took aim and fired twice. The noise was deafening, even though it was fake, and Amber jumped with a little squeak, but Rain took no notice. She missed one target, but managed to hit the other, and the instructor beamed his approval. 'Excellent, way to go. Right team, everyone will have five tries and I'm going to write down the scores to give to your teachers, so do your best, okay?'

Jesse, Zane and Mick had all used various types of guns before, so they managed to hit several birds each, while Cody missed every time. Jesse tried not to look at Zane when that happened, since he knew they'd both be tempted to laugh, which would be mean. Rain hit quite a few more, Dakota and Hayley hit one each, but Amber found the gun too heavy so her shots went wide.

'Never mind, you'll beat us all in archery, right?' Jesse said, trying to cheer her up as they made their way to the archery targets.

'I'd better, or else,' Amber muttered mulishly. 'Why does *she* have to be so damn good at everything? It must be because she's never had a social life so she's had plenty of time to practise other stuff.'

Jesse guessed that by 'she' Amber meant Rain, but he didn't comment. He was pretty sure Rain had had a very good social life back in England, and it annoyed him that Amber should assume anything about her. But he didn't want to discuss Rain at all so he kept his mouth zipped.

Their archery instructor used Amber to demonstrate the technique this time, and showing off her skill earned her lots of praise. She ate it up.

They all had a go, but Amber proved to be the best one until it was Rain's turn. Amber had scored four bullseyes out of five shots and was blatantly pleased with herself. Then Rain took aim and shot off two perfect arrows in a row plus one very close shot. Jesse saw Amber narrow her eyes and just as Rain was about to fire off arrow number four, Amber sneezed very loudly. Rain missed the bullseye by a fraction and sent Amber a murderous glance.

'Everyone keep quiet, please,' the instructor said, although he didn't seem to register the fact that Amber had sneezed on purpose. Jesse had though, and he frowned at her.

'What?' she whispered. 'I have hay fever.'

'In November? Yeah, right.'

Rain took aim again and prepared to shoot off her final arrow. Just before she let it fly, Amber gave a little shriek of terror. 'Aaargh! Daddy longlegs, get it off!' She flapped her hands and danced around, but Jesse couldn't see any insects within a ten-foot radius and grabbed her hands to stop her.

'Cut it out, Amber,' he hissed. 'That was cheating.'

'Was not. We can't let her be best at everything. She's already too stuck-up as it is.'

Jesse turned to look at Rain, who had missed this shot completely for obvious reasons, and saw her eyes shooting sparks at Amber, but to his surprise she didn't say anything, just handed the bow back to the instructor and marched off with Zane and Dakota. He was astonished that she hadn't made a scene. Any other girl on the planet would have thrown a hissy fit, but she just held her head high as if it didn't matter.

'She is not. Now come on,' Jesse said to Amber, not hiding his annoyance. 'I think we're doing tug-of-war now or something. At least you can't cheat in that.'

'It wasn't cheating. I can't help it if some insect from hell decides to attack me. Come on, Jesse, don't be mad. You don't want me to be humiliated, do you?'

Jesse didn't answer, just took her hand and pulled her along after the others. He was beginning to think that he *did* want her to be humiliated, and he didn't want to be that mean. He was feeling guilty enough already.

Tug-of-war sounded like a very childish thing to do, like Rain had said to Zane, but when it came down to it, everyone took it very seriously. Dr A had drawn a line in the dirt with a can of bright yellow spray paint and there was a thick rope with eight knots on either side for them to pull on.

'Come on, teams, line up now. I'd suggest you put the smallest person at the front, tallest and heaviest ones at the back. Alternate boy, girl if you can. That's it, get a move on.'

Zane acted as unofficial team leader and organised them into a line. Rain found to her dismay that she was second to last, with Zane in front of her and Jesse behind. That meant that she had to lean into Jesse when they pulled and that was the last thing she wanted to do. She didn't want to be anywhere near him.

'Ready, steady, PULL!' Dr A shouted, and pull they did, with all their strength.

At first Rain's efforts were a bit half-hearted, because that way she didn't have to lean on Jesse very much. She was extremely aware of him, but tried not to think about it and just closed her eyes and pretended to pull. He must have noticed however, because he muttered behind her, 'Come on, Rain, I'm not poisonous, you know. Put your back into it. I know you're stronger than that. We can win this easily.'

That did it. She decided to show him just how strong she was and began to pull with all her might. 'That's better,' he grunted, leaning forward so his face was buried somewhere in her hair. She tried not to notice the feel of his hard muscled thighs straining behind hers, which was very distracting, or his soft breath fanning her cheek from behind. It was driving her mad, but pretty soon they had the other team beaten and were through to the next round. Relieved, she stumbled off to sit on the ground for a moment, trying to make her body stop shaking.

This won't do. She had to get a grip on herself.

'Are you okay?' Jesse sat down next to her and she looked up in surprise. She had thought he'd try to avoid her as much as possible.

'Yes, I'm fine. Just catching my breath.'

'Right.' He stared at the ground. 'About the archery …'

'Forget it. If your girlfriend wants to win that badly, it doesn't matter. I couldn't care less.' And she didn't. She just wanted to go home. Or somewhere she didn't have to watch Jesse with Little-Miss-Perfect Amber.

'Okay. Well, thanks for not making a scene.' He stood up and walked off and Rain took a deep breath. This was going to be a very long day.

Their team eventually finished second, but by that time everyone was so hungry they didn't care. They all sat down on benches roughly hewn out of logs and tucked into whatever they'd brought. To Rain's relief, Jesse disappeared to sit with Amber and her friends on the other side of the clearing and she felt as if she could breathe again.

She pulled out her sandwiches from her backpack and relaxed, finally taking note of her surroundings. It was a beautiful day and the trees all around them were showing off the autumn colours New England was so famous for – reds, oranges, yellows and ochres. It really was pretty spectacular and made you happy to be alive. She told herself she should try to enjoy the day and stop obsessing about Jesse, but she still couldn't help glancing his way every now and again.

She scratched absently at her arm, where the tattoo was healing nicely, then stopped herself. *That won't help.* She'd had to cover it for today, which was making it itch more, and she was tempted to take her jacket off for a while and allow the skin to breathe. It wasn't quite warm enough though, so she decided against it.

'Man, we're good,' Zane said, looking pleased. 'We're lying second overall, so if we can just nail this orienteering business, we might win. Dr A said there'd be a great prize for the best team. Not sure what though.'

'I didn't know you were so competitive,' Rain teased. 'Does it really matter?'

'Hell, yeah! I hate losing.' But Zane was smiling, so Rain figured he wouldn't be heartbroken if they didn't win after all.

'The orienteering will be easy.' Cody spoke up in between mouthfuls of a huge BLT and the others turned to him in surprise. 'I've done it before, so I'll lead us to victory,' he announced confidently.

'Right, well, good. You'd better go get the instructions, then,' Zane said and Cody trooped off to collect their package, which consisted of a compass, a map and some other bits of paper.

'Want help reading that?' Mick offered.

Cody shook his head. 'I got this.' He bent over the map and seemed lost in contemplation, so the others left him to it.

Rain noticed that Cody seemed to be having some trouble with the compass and whispered to Zane, 'Are you sure we shouldn't give him a hand?'

Jesse, who had come back with a mulish Amber in tow, also sent Cody a worried glance and added, 'Yeah, he doesn't look too confident.'

'Ha! You ever been on the receiving end of his injured pride? I'll pass.'

'Okay, whatever. It can't be that difficult, right?'

Chapter Nineteen

'My feet are killing me, can we stop for a while please?' Amber sank down onto a fallen tree trunk with a moan.

'Amber, we stopped only five minutes ago.' Zane grabbed her arm and pulled her up. 'Come on, we've got to keep going. You shouldn't have worn new boots. That's the stupidest thing I've ever heard of.'

'Is not! They were perfectly comfortable when I tried them on in the shop.' She turned her doe-eyes on Jesse. 'Make them stop for a while, please? I just can't go on.'

Jesse shook his head. 'No, we can't, we've stopped too much already. Just quit complaining and actually walk for a change.'

'How dare you talk to me like that! You're supposed to be on my side.' Amber put her hands on her hips and glared at him. 'What kind of boyfriend are you if you can be that mean to me when I'm in pain?'

'Obviously not the kind you want.' Jesse gritted his teeth. Her whining had been getting on his nerves for the last hour and he'd just about reached the limit of his patience. He knew the others felt the same. And he was still pissed at her for cheating earlier, even if Rain hadn't seemed bothered.

'Damn right you're not.' Big fat tears hovered on her lashes. 'Well, if you can't treat me right, we're over, d'you hear me? I'm going to walk with Cody.'

Jesse took a deep breath. He knew she didn't mean it really, she was only trying to make him do as she wanted. But he'd had enough of her ultimatums and she was giving him an out. 'Okay, fine,' he said calmly. 'So we're over. Now let's go before it gets dark.'

'What?' Her squeak of outrage showed him he'd been

right, but he turned away. He wasn't going to give her the chance to change her mind.

'You jerk! You …' Amber started calling him names, but Zane took her hand and tugged her along towards Cody, muttering, 'Can we not do this now, please? This isn't helping.'

Amber turned on him instead. 'It's only because we've had to walk much further than anyone else that my feet hurt. Where are we anyway? Cody? You said you knew what you were doing.'

'We're nearly there,' Cody said, although he didn't sound as sure as he had an hour earlier. So far, they hadn't even found the first checkpoint. 'Come on, babe, I'll give you a piggyback for a bit,' he offered.

They had been walking for hours now and the forest seemed to have closed in around them. At first, they'd all just followed Cody without paying much attention to where they were going. Mick and Zane had kept up a joking conversation with all the girls, apart from Amber, and Jesse had been lost in his own world. Thoughts of what he'd found in the attic kept swirling around in his mind, and every time he glanced at Rain, thoughts of what had happened after the concert bugged him as well. Sunk in misery, he'd failed to notice the passing of time. Now he realised the afternoon was almost over, with no results, and he couldn't take any more of this. Since no one else was doing anything, he had to sort it out.

'No, we're not nearly there, actually,' Jesse said. 'We're completely lost. I knew we shouldn't have listened to you, Cody. You haven't got a clue how to follow a compass, do you? Admit it.'

'Shut it, Devlin!' Cody's face was bright red, embarrassment turning to anger.

'Whatever, man. It'll be getting dark soon, so you won't be able to see the damn compass anyway. Looks like we're going to have to build a campfire and just wait out the night or hope to be rescued. We'd better start collecting wood now, while we can still see.' Jesse looked around at the others in the group and saw a few reluctant nods. No one challenged his right to authority; they were all obviously fed up with Cody and his non-existent orienteering skills as well. Dusk was definitely falling and they didn't have a hope in hell of finding their way out before dark.

Rain had walked without complaining the whole afternoon, just like Hayley and Dakota, and Jesse couldn't help but compare their attitudes to that of Amber, who was still muttering in the background. Even Mick, who was usually so laid back he was almost horizontal, hissed at Amber to shut up. It made Jesse feel slightly better about breaking up with her in such a public way. That wasn't how he'd normally do things. *But what the hell – she asked for it!*

Zane, who was next to Jesse, said, 'Why don't we build some shelters too? That way we'll be warmer. It's going to get pretty cold during the night, isn't it?'

'What kind of shelters?' Rain, who'd seemed lost in thought, came over to stand with them. Jesse stared at her in surprise. She had avoided him all afternoon, as if she couldn't bear to be near him, which stung. But now she seemed to be talking to him again. He wondered if there was any chance they could be friends at least. He'd really missed having her around.

'You know, made of branches and stuff,' Zane clarified. 'My grandpa used to take me out in the forest when I was a little kid. He showed me how.'

'I know what you mean,' Rain put in and looked at the others. 'Didn't you guys play in the woods when you were little? And you must have the equivalent of the Duke of Edinburgh's Award over here, right? Or Scouts or something?'

'We don't have any weird awards, whatever that Duke thing is,' Cody sneered, 'and when I go camping with my family we always take a tent.'

'Yes, well, in case you hadn't noticed, we didn't bring any tents, although God knows we should've done with you as our guide,' Rain shot back. 'So we'll just have to do it the hard way. Come on, Zane, tell us what to do. Who else is helping?'

'I will,' Jesse said. He registered gratitude in her eyes, but it was quickly masked as other people volunteered to help as well. Everyone except Cody, who sat down on a fallen log and turned his head away, sulking, and Amber who complained of blisters and sat next to him, taking off her fancy pink boots and rubbing her feet. Cody seemed to be commiserating with her and Jesse heard him say something about a foot massage, but he couldn't care less. Cody could do whatever the hell he wanted with Amber if it saved Jesse from dealing with her.

Zane took charge. 'Okay. First, we need to find some stout branches in the shape of a Y.'

Rain looked around and spotted a suitable bush. 'Like this one?'

'Yes, exactly.' Zane smiled at her. 'Someone break that off, please.'

Jesse obliged and soon several similar branches were found. Zane showed them how to hammer them into the ground with a large stone so they stood upright. A longer branch was found to lie on top to form a frame like a goal post, then other shorter Y-shaped branches were leaned against the back making the outline of half a tent.

'Now we weave some hazel or other soft twigs through these, then we need plenty of fir or pine tree branches, really bushy ones, to thread in on top. After that, we cover the whole thing with fern fronds, moss and anything else we can find with big leaves on.'

'How about some moss and dried leaves and stuff to go inside?' Dakota suggested. 'That should insulate us from the cold ground a bit.'

'Good idea. We could even lie down, then.' Zane winked at Dakota, who blushed pink. 'Anyone got a pocket knife? I've got one, but two would be faster.'

'Yeah, I brought one,' Jesse said.

'And me,' Mick added.

Everyone followed orders without complaining and Jesse had to admit the result was pretty good. It probably wouldn't stand up to any severe gales or heavy rain, but it was protection from the wind and with a fire going in front of the opening, they should be cosy enough.

He and Rain worked side by side and somehow they were able to talk to each other again, almost like before the concert. It felt good and raised Jesse's spirits. He felt a spark of hope. *Maybe she doesn't hate me after all?* Maybe he'd just handled things badly and now was his chance to do it better?

'Let's build a fire just outside here and another shelter on the other side of it, that way we should be able to keep fairly warm,' he suggested. 'This one's only big enough for four of us at the most.'

'Good thinking.' Rain smiled her approval and he drew in a hissing breath. She hadn't smiled at him like that for weeks now and he'd missed it so much it hurt. Suddenly, she seemed like the old Rain again, the one who'd sung with him and written songs with him. He turned away to hide the warm glow it gave him to think she might have changed her mind, although he didn't dare hope too much.

When the second shelter was finished, they built a ring of stones and got a good fire going inside it. There was plenty of dry wood all around them and there was no problem lighting it since Jesse had brought the matches. They split into two groups, four people in each, and sat inside the shelters on top of a soft, springy bed of moss, ferns and piles of dead leaves. Dakota and Zane sat down in one together, and Rain and Jesse joined them. He ignored the glare he received from Amber, who had no choice but to sit on the other side of the fire with Cody, Hayley and Mick.

'Hey, this is kind of cool,' Dakota said with a giggle, leaning into Zane as he put his arm round her shoulders. 'Now all we need is some food. Who's going to go catch our dinner?'

'Euwww!' Amber shuddered. 'I'm not eating anything anyone's killed. I'd rather starve.'

'You always starve, you should be used to it,' Zane muttered, but thankfully Amber didn't hear him.

'Yeah, well, you might have to because I don't think we have anything much left to eat,' Jesse said. He looked across the fire and wondered what he'd ever seen in her. She was such a spoiled pain in the backside. Sure, she was pretty, but only on the outside. Thank God they were over.

It had been hours since they'd eaten their packed lunches and Jesse's stomach grumbled at the thought, but he knew there wasn't anything he could do about it. No one would die from going without food for one night, even if it was uncomfortable.

'I'm sure we all must have some stuff left over from earlier. I have some cookies,' Hayley said, and brought out a crumpled package. 'Let's all share whatever we've got.'

Jesse remembered his Oreos and pulled them out. 'Half a pack of these left,' he said.

Mick dug in his bag. 'Cheetos!'

'An apple?' Dakota brought out a Tupperware box with apple slices. 'Oh, yeah, and some Hershey's Kisses.'

'And I have chocolate too,' Rain added. 'I always bring extra supplies if I'm going to be outdoors all day.'

'Another Duke-of-whatsit idea?' Jesse teased, but he sent her an approving look to show he didn't mean to annoy her.

'Of course,' she said. 'Or Scout maybe – be prepared?' She opened her backpack and took out four big Mars bars.

'Okay, you guys, let's share it out.' Dakota took charge of this and everyone was given a strange assortment of food. 'Hey, I like this kind of diet,' she added with a grin.

'I hate Mars bars, so sticky. And all those carbs and sugar, yuck,' Amber grumbled, while nibbling on a cookie, which was all she seemed to want.

'Then I'll have yours,' Cody said greedily, and Amber just shrugged. 'I don't have any food left over,' he continued, 'but I do have something even better.' He pulled a thermos flask out of his rucksack. 'Irish coffee!'

'You're kidding?' Jesse couldn't believe Cody had brought alcohol on a field trip.

'Sure, why not? I knew I'd get cold at some point. Want some?'

'Er, no thanks.' Jesse didn't like whisky much. It reminded him of the way Tom reeked whenever he came home from the bar.

'I'll have a sip,' Mick said, and took a swig, then coughed and wheezed. 'Jesus, man, that's more Irish than coffee!'

Cody just grinned. 'So maybe I spiked it a little too much, but that's good, right?'

'Nah, you keep it.' Mick made a face.

'Er, should we maybe save half the food for the morning, in case we don't find our way out straight away?' Jesse asked.

'No, it's okay, I have a few more Mars bars,' Rain said. 'Enough for breakfast anyway.'

Jesse raised his eyebrows at her. 'I'm seriously impressed.'

She shrugged. 'It's no big.'

He chuckled. 'My stomach thinks it is. I have some extra water if anyone wants?' He passed the bottles around.

'Although we can probably find somewhere to fill them up if we need to. The water out here should be pretty clean, right?'

They sat in their shelters talking and telling stupid jokes for a while until it was completely dark all around them. Jesse was very aware of Rain sitting next to him, their shoulders so close they touched every time one of them moved. He wondered if she was aware of it too, or if he left her cold. The kisses they'd shared had shown him that she had plenty of passion, but he didn't know if it could ever be aimed at him again. She'd probably just been mad then and trying to beat him at his own game. It was a lowering thought. *And it worked too, damn it!*

'Anyone bring any music?' Zane asked. 'You're meant to sing round a campfire, aren't you?' He looked at Jesse. 'Shame you don't have your guitar.'

'Oh, please.' Amber rolled her eyes. 'How cheesy is that?'

'I think it's a great idea,' Dakota spoke up. 'Let's all sing something. How about the Beatles? Everyone knows those.'

They started off a bit hesitantly, but soon grew raucous, especially whenever Cody joined in, which he did all too frequently. Jesse wondered how much whisky they guy had drunk, but figured it wasn't his problem. Zane hammed it up, as always playing the clown, so some of the tunes degenerated into chaos, but that just made everyone laugh so it didn't matter. At least it passed the time.

Eventually everyone started yawning.

'So what's the best way to keep warm, do you think?' Zane asked, hugging Dakota close with a suggestive wiggle of his eyebrows. 'I hear shared body heat is the thing for keeping people alive in extreme conditions.'

Dakota giggled, but gave him a little pretend push of outrage. 'Zane!'

'What does the Duke of thingie expert say?' Zane challenged Rain.

'I wouldn't say I'm an expert precisely, but I have to admit you're kind of right, although not in the way that you think.'

'Huh?' Zane's face was a picture of confusion. He had obviously expected her to tell him to shut up and stop with the sexual innuendoes.

Rain laughed. 'What I mean is, you're right about the shared body heat, but you need to keep your clothes on, at least some of them. I suggest we pair up and take our jackets off. If we put one underneath us and one on top and then snuggle together to share the warmth, that should do the trick. At least, that's what I read in a book once. We'd be much colder lying straight onto the ground, I should think.'

Jesse nodded. 'That makes sense to me. Let's do it.' He started to take off his jacket.

'I can't take mine off,' Amber protested from across the fire. 'I haven't got anything underneath.'

'What, nothing?' Cody stared at her with definite interest and she glared at him.

'Well, a small top obviously, but that's it. Don't go getting any ideas.'

To Jesse's surprise, Rain took off her jacket, then pulled off one of her fleece sweaters and handed it to Amber. 'Here, you can borrow this. I'll be fine with one. I have a thermal vest thingie underneath.'

Amber looked as if she was going to refuse at first, but then she shivered which must have made her realise this wasn't the time to consider fashion or rivalry. 'Thanks,' she muttered, and took off her jacket so she could put the fleece on. Jesse had to bite back a sharp comment when he saw the skimpy top underneath. What on earth had she been thinking?

'Jesse, can I talk to you for a minute?' Amber jumped to her feet and hovered in between the two shelters. 'Please?'

Jesse hesitated, because he could guess what was coming,

but then he figured he owed her that much anyway. He stood up and didn't protest when she pulled him out of earshot of the others.

'What?' He put his hands in his jacket pockets and kept his distance.

'Look, I'm sorry about earlier,' she began, 'but I really thought you were out of line. Still, I'm prepared to forgive you. I know we all had a rough day and you were probably hungry. I know how grumpy you get when you don't get fed.' She put her hand on his arm and moved closer. 'But I want you to keep me warm now, you're so big and strong. So are we good?'

He pulled away from her. 'Actually, no, Amber, we're not. I don't think I *am* the right boyfriend for you, you were right about that,' Jesse said firmly. 'Besides, Rain is more my size, so it makes sense to pair up with her, otherwise I'll be cold too. You share with Cody, he's plenty big enough for you and he has a huge padded jacket.'

'What? No way! You can't mean that.'

'Yes, I do, I'm sorry. Now come on, let's go get some sleep. I'm beat.' He turned away to indicate the discussion was at an end.

'How can you be so heartless? And no one, no one, do you hear me,' she hissed while poking him in the back, 'breaks up with me. I do the breaking up.'

'You did, Amber, remember? You said it, not me.'

Jesse walked back to the shelter and pretended he didn't hear the outraged squeak, nor Amber stomping back to fling herself down next to Cody.

'Ow, watch it! Or are you trying to sit on my lap? Here, I don't mind, not one bit.'

Amber must have hit Cody, because muffled curses and complaints came from the opposite shelter until Cody lost his temper. 'Aw, just shut up and lie down, then,' Jesse heard him say, adding, 'Call this a jacket? It's more like a handkerchief. Hell, how's this going to keep us warm?'

Dakota and Zane had already followed Rain's instructions and had bedded down at the back of the shelter. There were kissing noises coming from that direction, so Jesse figured they were keeping fairly warm at least. No worries there, and as he glanced across the fire, he saw Hayley and Mick looking fairly snug too. Rain's plan was working out well so far, apart from Cody and Amber who still seemed to be having a tussle over whose jacket should go on top and whose underneath them. Amber's really was so small, it barely covered one of them.

Jesse felt a twinge of guilt, but suppressed it. He couldn't face lying next to Amber now, he just couldn't. They were finished and he didn't want anything more to do with her.

Rain wasn't looking at Jesse, but she'd put her jacket on the ground. 'I think yours is bigger so will be better on top,' she muttered by way of an explanation, 'if … if you're staying over here.'

'Yeah, I am and you're right. Hang on, I'm just going to put some more wood on the fire to keep it going. Just in case any wild animals get ideas about eating us during the night or something.'

He could hear more whispered arguing from the shelter opposite, but ignored it. If she wanted to keep warm, Amber had no choice but to co-operate with Cody and it was their problem how they achieved this. Jesse found he couldn't care less.

When he turned back, Rain was already lying down on top of her jacket, curled up on her side. He stepped over her and lay down behind her, draping his coat over the two of them and tucking it in to make a sort of cocoon. Finally, he put one arm tentatively round Rain's stomach and pulled her back against his front. 'How's that?' he asked quietly.

'Good,' she said, her voice sounding a bit huskier than usual, as if she was embarrassed.

'You don't mind sharing with me?' he whispered. 'I mean, I didn't even ask. Sorry. I know I'm not exactly your favourite person at the moment and all.'

'No, it's okay. You were right about our sizes matching. I'm not a tiny doll like Amber.'

He hugged her closer. 'You heard that, huh? Don't do yourself down. You're just right, tall and graceful, but not too tall. At least not for me.'

'Er ... thank you.'

Jesse didn't want to spook her, so he didn't say anything else for a while. Instead, he just held her close and felt the heat spread where their bodies touched.

She felt good to hold as well. *So good.* He closed his eyes and enjoyed the sensation. He couldn't remember the last time anything had felt so right. If only they could stay this way forever.

Chapter Twenty

Rain lay completely still at first, wondering what Jesse had meant when he said she was just the right size for him. She was astonished he had decided to share with her, and even more amazed he'd finished with his girlfriend today of all days. But although she was secretly thrilled by this development, it was also a bit awkward. After all, she didn't know if he was just temporarily pissed off with Amber, or if he'd really meant it was over for good.

She had noticed him becoming more and more irritated with Amber as the day wore on, and she was glad he'd finally had his eyes opened to what the girl was really like. Normally Amber was all sweetness and light around Jesse, but today she'd shown her true colours. Rain could only hope Jesse didn't fall under Amber's spell again when they got back to civilisation. There was no way Rain could compete with Amber under normal circumstances. And she knew now that she wanted to compete. She shouldn't have given up so easily.

She relaxed and wriggled a bit closer towards Jesse. Well, she had him right now and would have to make the most of it. They fit together like two matching spoons and he was lovely and warm. She felt him adjust his grip around her middle and then, to her delight, he buried his face in her hair just beneath her ear, almost knocking her hat off. It tickled a bit, so she wriggled again and tried not to giggle. 'Jesse!' she protested, half-heartedly, but she liked it and didn't want him to stop.

'I'm just warming my nose,' he whispered.

'Sure you are.'

'Turn around for a minute and I'll warm yours.'

Curious, she turned so she lay facing him. 'What? How are you going to do that?' She noticed he hadn't let go of her. Instead, his arm was now round her back and he pushed her gently so their bodies touched all the way down.

'Like this,' he breathed and kissed the tip of her nose.

'Oh.' Rain couldn't think of anything more intelligent to reply, but she was saved from having to say anything because in the next instant he put his mouth on hers, silencing her completely.

It was a gentle kiss at first, asking permission this time, as if he wasn't sure she wanted him to do this. Rain did hesitate for a fraction of a second, thinking of Amber lying just on the other side of the fire. But then she reasoned that surely he wouldn't be kissing someone else if he hadn't meant to break up with her? This must mean he was finished with her for good.

Giving in to what she'd wanted for so long, Rain kissed him back almost fiercely, to show him without words that this was definitely what she wanted. He got the message and she could feel him smile against her mouth.

He managed to get both arms around her and their kisses deepened. His tongue playing with hers felt just right. Not savage and punishing as it had done last time, but soft and yet demanding in a thrilling way. She couldn't get enough of him or his kisses. It was as if she'd been starved her whole life and now she had finally been given what she'd been longing for. He tasted of Mars bar and smelled of the fresh outdoors. She loved it.

It was heaven.

Rain had no idea how long they made out for, and since they had all night, she didn't care. But in the end he stopped and just held her tightly while their breathing slowed down a bit and their hearts stopped beating quite so frantically. 'I ... uhm, think we'd better cool it a bit,' he whispered, then added with a chuckle, 'I don't know about you, but I'm plenty warm enough right now.'

She had her arms round him now too and snuggled into him. 'Yes, you're right. Maybe we should try to sleep a little?'

'Good idea.'

'I'll turn around again, I think we'll be more comfortable that way.'

'Okay, but if I get cold later, can we ... er, do that again?'

'Of course.'

Smiling into the darkness, Rain made herself comfortable with her back against him once more. She was asleep within moments.

Jesse heard Rain's breathing become even and felt her body relax. He lay still so he wouldn't wake her, but he didn't want to sleep yet. He needed to think about what had just happened.

He had only meant to give her a tiny kiss, to see what her reaction would be and because it was really tempting with her so close, but he'd gotten more than he bargained for. A lot more. That tiny kiss had turned into something altogether more serious. It was as if a volcano had erupted inside him and he couldn't stop. Didn't want to stop. He wanted to go on kissing her for the rest of the night. That and more, but he knew he shouldn't think like that.

He could still hear rustling noises from across the fire and felt another stab of guilt, but he knew without a doubt that he didn't want Amber any more. He was going to ask Rain to date him instead, at least for as long as she stayed in the States. He could hardly believe he'd been given this second chance. But he was determined not to blow it this time. There could be no other girl for him now.

He breathed in the fresh smell of her hair and buried his face in it again. He loved her hair, it was so thick and beautiful and soft. And there was such a lot of it. The best thing about it, though, was that it was natural. Not crimped to within an inch of its life like Amber's, which was never allowed to have so much as a tiny curl out of place and always felt stiff to touch, with all the hairspray and other crap she put in it. Rain's hair just hung in a long curtain down her back or she twisted it into an untidy knot on top of her head, which looked damned sexy. He realised he wanted her to do that just so he could release it and watch it cascade down her back.

Damn, he wished she hadn't gone to sleep. He wanted to kiss her some more now. Maybe later she'd wake up and … He would just have to be patient. After tomorrow, if they could find their way back home, he'd be able to kiss her as much as he wanted to, hopefully somewhere a bit more private.

Perhaps if he waited a little bit longer he could wake her for a while? He didn't think she'd mind. *Yeah, I'll definitely do that.*

The forest was so quiet, Jesse could hear everyone starting to snore around him. He was just about dozing off himself when he heard a scuffle and some whispering from the other shelter. He lifted his head so he could catch what was being said.

'Aw, come on. Let me warm you, if you're so cold. You know you want me to.'

'No! Get your hands off of me, you jerk. I said no! Mm-hmmph, ergh!'

The scuffles increased and Jesse could just about make out a large shape on top of a smaller one, who seemed to be struggling. *Shit! What the hell is Cody doing?*

Jesse carefully wriggled out from under the jacket he was sharing with Rain, and although she stirred a little, she didn't wake up. Climbing over her, he stepped out of the shelter and across to the other side of the fire, where there were now muffled sounds of distress. He thought he heard a sob. It was pretty dark, but it looked to Jesse as if Cody was kissing Amber against her will and she was trying to push him off. Of course, being so small, she didn't have a hope in hell of doing that.

Why hasn't Mick noticed anything? But then Mick was known for being able to sleep through just about anything short of a bomb blast. Jesse bent down and grabbed Cody by the back of his sweater, rolling him off Amber and onto the ground outside the shelter.

'What the fuck do you think you're doing?' he hissed, still reluctant to wake the others. It might be better to keep this between themselves.

Cody twisted around and lashed out at him with a fist. 'Let go of me! This is none of your business. You broke up, remember?'

'Yeah, well, that doesn't mean I want Amber hurt. And it's pretty obvious she doesn't want you to touch her.'

'You're just sore cause you're over.' Cody's voice was a bit slurred and Jesse guessed he was still drunk. He got to his feet and pushed Jesse hard in the chest with both hands. 'Shouldn't have let her go.'

Jesse pushed back. 'You're a douche and you're drunk. Leave her alone.'

Cody tried to punch him, but missed and only hit Jesse's arm. 'White trash,' he taunted, something Jesse had heard a lot when he was younger just because his parents didn't have much money. It made him see red and he hit back.

The fight that followed was silent apart from grunts of pain and effort, but filled with simmering anger. As it was so dark, it was difficult to judge where to land blows, so Jesse grabbed onto Cody with one hand and hit with the other. Cody did the same and they were locked together, raining repeated blows on each other. The whisky seemed to fuel Cody's strength, so he was hitting pretty hard, but it also made him unsteady and not very accurate, which was in Jesse's favour. Plus Jesse was bigger. Finally, Jesse had enough and managed to land an upper cut on Cody's jaw, which sent him sprawling onto the ground.

Jesse bent over him and grabbed a fistful of his shirt, pushed him into the moss, and snarled, 'Don't touch Amber again unless she asks you. Understand?'

'I have a right to—'

'No, you don't. She decides. End of.'

Still holding Cody's shirt, Jesse gave him a rough shake and he subsided at last. 'Okay, fine, have it your way, but she was just playing hard to get.'

'I w-wasn't.'

Jesse turned to find that Amber had come up behind him and was standing there with her arms wrapped around herself. He felt sorry for her and after one last warning push, he let go of Cody and wrapped an arm round Amber's shoulders. 'Come on, let's go sit down somewhere. Are you okay?'

He steered her away from the campfire, which had died down anyway. He saw heads sticking out of the shelters and guessed the others had woken up, but he'd have to explain to them later. For now, he had to calm Amber down. She was shaking and he heard her teeth chattering.

'You've had a shock. Sit here.'

He pulled her onto a log and she leaned her head against his shoulder. 'Th-thank you.'

'No problem. Cody was way out of line, but I don't think he'll bother you again.'

They sat quietly for a bit and her shaking subsided. Jesse started to get cold as he wasn't wearing his jacket, and she wasn't either. 'Do you want me to get your jacket?' he asked.

'No, I'll get it in a minute.'

'Would you like to sleep between me and Zane? I think we can fit one more person in our shelter.'

'Maybe in a bit. I-I just want to sit here for a while. Calm down, you know?'

'Okay, I'll leave you to it.' Jesse stood up. 'Just come on over when you're ready.'

'Right. Won't you ... won't you stay with me now?'

Jesse hesitated. He wasn't sure if she was using this whole thing as an excuse to get close to him again. Of course she was shaken, but she'd calmed down now and there was nothing more he could do for her. *I've already offered her shelter with us. And I'm not her boyfriend any more.*

'No, Amber, I'm going to get some sleep. Don't stay here too long. Come join us.'

He turned and went back to the shelter, crawling in behind Rain. She felt wonderfully warm and to his relief she didn't say anything. She seemed to understand that he didn't want to talk about what had just happened. Not yet.

On the other side of the fire Cody had bedded down and was snoring like a pig. *Good!* Jesse closed his eyes.

They were all woken just after first light by the barking of dogs. Seconds later Rain looked up into a huge hairy muzzle and recoiled, but the big dog only gave an excited yap and thankfully backed off.

'What the hell ...?' Jesse muttered behind her.

'I think we've been found,' Rain told him. And soon after, the clearing was suddenly full of people. *A search party.* Rain felt guilty as she realised they'd probably been out looking for them all night. *And here we were, as snug and safe as anything!*

Everyone started to emerge from the shelters into the pale morning light, stiff and shivering, jumping up and down to get their circulation going. The air was so cold their breaths came out in plumes of mist, but because of their shelters and sharing body heat, no one was truly freezing.

No one except Amber.

'Over here! This one needs help,' Rain heard one of the rescue team call out. Jesse had been one of the last to emerge, looking very sleepy, and he hardly seemed to register what was happening until he looked over to where people were clustered round Amber. Rain heard him mutter, 'Shit!', then he sprinted to join the group.

'Is she okay? Amber! Wake up.'

'C-can't. S-s-so c-cold.'

Amber was sitting slouched on the ground with her back against a log. Rain noticed that Amber's face was ashen and she was shivering like crazy. Her teeth chattered against each other and she was only wearing Rain's fleece. No jacket, no hat, no scarf. *Oh, no* ... Rain felt an icy feeling of dread grope her stomach as she watched Amber's whole body convulse with trembling, as if she couldn't stop even if she wanted to.

'Oh, hell,' Rain muttered. Amber must have fallen asleep where she was instead of coming to their shelter after the kerfuffle in the middle of the night, and now the girl was frozen stiff. *This is not good.*

She saw Jesse shoot a look of fury at Cody, as if to say that this was all his fault. Cody was looking sulky again and kicked at a turf of grass with his hands in his pockets, but he didn't say anything. Rain had guessed what had happened, even though she'd been asleep through part of the events, but there hadn't been any point discussing it last night. Cody had to feel partly responsible though, unless he was completely brainless.

The rescue team were dealing with Amber and had her covered in special thermal blankets that looked like foil. 'Hang on, we'll get you home soon,' one of them said.

Someone else told them all to get ready to go, and soon they were walking through the woods, following two excited dogs and a man who seemed to know exactly where he was going.

Jesse insisted on taking turns with the rescue guys to help carry the stretcher they'd put Amber on. He'd put his coat on top of her to add to the layer of blankets, but since he was having to work hard, Rain figured he wouldn't be cold anyway. So far this morning, he'd hardly looked at Rain and now he seemed to be focused entirely on Amber. It was understandable, she reasoned with herself, but couldn't help feeling just a little bit hurt anyway. She turned away from the sight of him staring anxiously down at Amber, not wanting to see the expression on his face. If he was that worried about her, he obviously still had feelings for her.

So much for last night, Rain thought, and set off, her jaw clenched tight with frustration. *The sooner we're out of this forest, the faster I can go home and forget last night ever happened.*

They walked for about an hour, although to Jesse it must have felt longer since he was working so hard. Zane and Mick both offered to take their turn, but Jesse just shook his head. 'Nah, I'm fine. She doesn't weigh much.'

Rain felt a stab of jealousy, but knew she had no right to think that way. Amber had been his girlfriend for a long time, after all, and what had happened last night was obviously just a bit of fun for him in order to keep them warmer. He looked very concerned right now, and he had cause to be. Hypothermia could be fatal and there was no saying how long Amber had sat on the ground.

To Rain's relief, they emerged onto a road at last and

started walking south. There had been no signal on any of their mobiles the day before, deep inside the forest, but after walking another five minutes or so along the road, Zane shouted, 'Yes, it's working again! Shall I call for help?'

But the rescue team had walkie-talkies and had already taken care of it. It wasn't long before they could hear the sound of the ambulance siren and soon afterwards Amber was being loaded into the back, together with Jesse.

'You'd better come with her,' one of the ambulance men ordered. 'We'll need someone who can speak for her, if she's not up to it.'

'Okay.' Jesse looked as if he wanted to protest, but in the end he did as he was told. Rain turned away. She couldn't bear to watch him leave with Amber, but just before she did so, she saw Amber reach for Jesse's hand. He didn't resist.

A minibus turned up eventually to take the rest of them home. It was a tired, subdued group and hardly anyone spoke except to tell the teachers their story. Rain and the others were congratulated on their presence of mind and survival skills, but she let the others reply on her behalf. She really didn't care.

She just wanted Jesse.

Chapter Twenty-One

The whole group were given Friday off to recuperate, although Rain knew they were all fine really and could have gone to school. She couldn't settle to anything and spent the time just listening to music, reading, e-mailing or watching DVDs. Saturday passed the same way, with no word from anyone apart from Hayley and Dakota. They talked of nothing other than Mick and Zane, however, so eventually Rain just turned off her mobile and she sank further and further into misery.

On Sunday afternoon her mother tried to make her go with her parents to a neighbouring town for a party at some friends' house, but Rain refused.

'Sorry, Mum, but I'm still really tired from that outing and my head hurts a bit.' The last part was definitely a lie, but Lady Mackenzie believed her.

'All right, then, darling, you stay here and recuperate. Are you sure you'll be okay on your own?'

'I'll be fine. I'm just going to rest.'

It was blessedly peaceful after her parents had left. Rain knew they meant well, but they had been fussing over her since her return and it was getting on her nerves. After all, nothing had happened to her other than the fact that she'd had to spend a night in the forest. She'd been as warm as toast, thanks to Jesse.

'Aargh!' She groaned out loud. She really didn't want to think about him any more. There was no point. He was probably with Amber at the hospital, agreeing to her every whim, and that was not something she wanted to dwell on.

She showered and washed her hair, then watched yet another DVD – a soppy teenage movie that made her even more miserable because the lead actor and actress got it together in the end. Afterwards she went to the kitchen to fetch a tub of chocolate ice cream to console herself with. She was just making her way back to the sitting room when the doorbell went.

At first she considered not answering it, but then she decided she had better in case it was something important to do with her dad's business interests. When she looked through the peephole, however, her heart began to beat frantically. It was Jesse.

She opened the door a fraction, wishing she'd put on some mascara, although she had naturally black eyelashes and knew she didn't really need it. 'Er, hello,' she said. 'What are you doing here?'

He looked a bit tense and stood with his hands in his pockets. 'I just wanted to talk to you for a sec. Can I come in?'

'Um, I guess. I'm not really dressed for visitors.' She opened the door wider and let him in, cringing as he took in her skimpy T-shirt and baggy old tracksuit bottoms.

He waited while she closed the door behind him, then hesitated before saying, 'Can we maybe go up to your room? I'd like to talk to you in private.'

'It's okay, my parents are out for the evening. It's just me here.'

'Oh, right, okay.'

'Come in to the lounge. I was just watching some DVDs.' She led the way after he shed his jacket in the hall. When she sat down on the sofa, he seated himself next to her instead of on the opposite one, which was a bit disconcerting. To stop herself thinking about how close he was, Rain opened the ice cream tub and absent-mindedly put a spoonful in her mouth.

He gave her a small smile. 'Are you sharing?'

'Huh? Oh, the ice cream. Sorry. I don't know what I was thinking. I'll get you a bowl and spoon.' She stood up to go back to the kitchen, but he reached out and grabbed her arm, pulling her down again gently.

'No, it's okay. I was just kidding and anyway, I can eat from the tub same as you, unless you're scared of my cooties? A bit late for that though, I'd say.'

Rain realised he was referring to all the kisses they'd shared and felt herself blush a deep scarlet. *Damn, why did he have to mention that?* To cover her embarrassment, she loaded a spoon up and held it out to him. 'You're right. Here.'

He ate the ice cream, licking his top lip where she managed to smear some. She couldn't take her eyes off his mouth and swallowed hard. Adopting a very fake, cheerful kind of voice, she said, 'So how's Amber?'

'Better. The doctors are letting her go home this afternoon and she's going to be fine, or so I'm told. That's kind of why I came. We're over, you know.'

Rain forced a laugh. 'We never really started, so there wasn't any need for you to tell me that,' she said brightly, taking another spoonful of ice cream just so she wouldn't have to look at him.

'No, you don't understand. I mean, me and Amber are over, definitely.'

'What? Really?' Rain swallowed abruptly and almost choked on the cold lump that slid down her throat un-chewed. She stared at Jesse.

'The thing is, they wouldn't let me see her until this morning, so I had to wait to speak to her until today. I didn't think it was right to ask someone else to be my girlfriend until I'd made sure she understood I wasn't going to change my mind about her. She kept babbling on about it in the ambulance, saying she'd known I hadn't meant it and all this kind of stuff. But I only carried her because I felt guilty about not making sure she came back to the shelter to keep warm. Anyway, I had no idea it was going to take so long before I could talk to her. In fact, it's been the longest two days of my life.' He ran his fingers through his hair, making it stand up even more than usual.

'Your girlfriend?' Rain echoed, feeling as if this whole scenario was unreal.

He smiled and reached out to stroke her cheek. 'Yeah, I want you to be my girlfriend instead of Amber, at least for however long you're staying here. I figure any time with you would be better than none. I didn't know how you'd feel about that though and it's just about killed me to wait this long to find out. So what do you say?'

'I ... I ... Hell, yes!'

Jesse laughed and took the ice cream tub away from her and put it on a nearby table. 'You'll date me and no one else, until you leave?'

'Absolutely. I mean, I'd love to. That is ... if you're sure that's what you want?' Rain couldn't believe this was happening. Could she really be that lucky? Jesse was the most gorgeous guy she'd ever met and he was asking her to date him exclusively.

He nodded. 'It's what I want more than anything – since I first saw you, I think.'

'Well, good, but I should probably tell you I'm not planning on leaving now. So you might have to put up with me for longer than you thought. This place has kind of grown on me.'

He let out a whoop of delight. 'That's the best news I've heard in a long time. I don't want you to leave, ever. Come here.' He pulled her close and bent to kiss her, tenderly at first, then more demanding. He groaned. 'God, I thought I'd never get to do that again and it was all I could think of.' He kissed her again, pulling her down on the sofa. Rain twined her arms round his neck and closed her eyes. This was Paradise.

When they had to stop to breathe for a while, she asked, 'You really want me instead of Amber? I can't believe it.'

'Well, you'd better, because that's the way it is. Amber may be nice to look at, but she's not that great on the inside. I should have finished with her a long time ago, but it just seemed easier not to, somehow. Plus, I have to admit it gave me a kind of status to be her boyfriend just because everyone else wanted her too. Stupid, huh? Anyway, they're all welcome to her now.'

'But why me? I'm nothing special. In fact, I thought you considered me a right pain as well.'

'Are you kidding? Actually, maybe I did to begin with, but you got under my skin and I couldn't stop thinking about you. And after you did that concert with us, I knew I'd fallen in love with you, but then I messed up ...'

'You love me?' The wonder of it almost took her breath away.

'Sure I do. Why, don't you love me? Cause if you don't, I've no idea what you're doing on this sofa with me.' He grinned at her, teasingly.

'Of course I do, but guys don't always admit things like that. Or so I thought.'

'Well, I'm not ashamed to admit it. You're the best thing that's ever happened to me and you're absolutely gorgeous. Just the right size for me. In fact, I love everything about you.'

He tangled his fingers in her hair and kissed her again, and this time it lasted even longer. As far as Rain was concerned, it could last forever.

Epilogue

November the twenty-fourth, his birthday, passed in a strange blur for Jesse while he did what he'd always said he would – packed up all his stuff to move out of his dad's house. *No, Tom's house.* He had been offered a small room to rent by one of the guys he worked with at the garage, and although it wouldn't leave him much cash, he'd accepted. Now all he had to do was tell Tom he was leaving.

By six o'clock, his possessions were loaded into the Mustang, his room was clean and he sat by the kitchen table, waiting. Tom usually came home around this time, so he knew the confrontation would be over soon. He felt kind of sad that it had come to this, but he had decided this was the only way. The two of them would never see eye to eye and he was tired of having to hide out in his room just to avoid Tom's violent moods. He just hoped there wouldn't be a fight today because he had promised Rain he'd have dinner with her and her parents to celebrate their joint birthday and he didn't want to arrive all bloodstained and bruised.

The question was, should he tell Tom he knew about his real father? Or didn't it matter?

'What're you sitting here for?' Tom demanded, the minute he walked in. 'Shouldn't you be out celebrating with your friends or something?'

Jesse noticed Tom didn't say happy birthday, although he obviously knew what day it was. He hadn't expected a card or any presents, but a couple of words surely wouldn't hurt? 'I'll be doing that later,' he said quietly. 'First, I wanted to tell you I'm leaving and I'm not coming back.'

Tom nodded. 'Figured that. Well, good, have a nice life, kid.'

Jesse stared at him, his mouth almost falling open. 'Is that all you have to say? Your son is leaving for good and you say "have a nice life"?' He couldn't believe even Tom Devlin could be that callous. He may not be Tom's real son, but they had shared a home for all of Jesse's life. For all intents and purposes, they'd been family.

Tom snorted. 'Well, now you're old enough, guess I might as well tell you the truth. You ain't my son and never have been. Your mama cheated me. She hooked up with some rocker dude and got herself in the family way, but she didn't tell me that until after I married her. She had me down for a sucker and I sure was.'

Jesse nodded. 'I know,' he said quietly.

'You do, huh? Well, you should'a said.'

'Why didn't you?' It was the one thing Jesse wanted to know most of all. Why had Tom played the role of father all these years if he hated it so much? 'When Mom died and … you could have told me then.' He didn't understand.

'Didn't want the neighbours to find out. That would've been embarrassing. Don't want people to know what a schmuck I was. I figured you'd take off soon as you could anyhow, so no need for anyone to know any different.'

Jesse shook his head. It seemed like a dumb reason to him, but if he looked at it from Tom's point of view, it was a question of pride. And Tom had always been a proud man, never asking anyone for anything. 'So you knew who my real dad was then?'

Tom shrugged. 'Like I said, some rocker in a band your mom liked. Lizard? Cobra? No, something like that. She said his first name was Rick.'

'Snake,' Jesse muttered.

'Yeah, that's the one.' Tom nodded. 'Not that he'd care one way or another. She was probably just one in a long line of women for him, stupid bitch.'

Normally Jesse would have defended his mother. He

hated it when Tom talked about her like she was dirt, but he'd had a lot of time to think about this and in a way, he knew Tom was probably right. Lily hadn't played fair. She'd been in love with Rick Linden, but she'd known someone like that wouldn't marry a small town girl like her. Her letter had said she'd wanted a father for her son, but Jesse felt she should have at least told Tom up front that she'd been pregnant. *No wonder he was angry!* Still, Jesse didn't have the energy to argue about it right now. *What does it matter?*

Jesse stared at Tom one more time, then nodded at him. 'Well, I won't say thank you for looking after me, because you didn't, but you put a roof over my head and paid for the food, and now I can go without feeling guilty, so thank you for that.'

Tom shrugged again and went over to the fridge to get out a beer. 'Go, then,' he said. 'Get out of my sight. I've got a game to watch on TV.'

'Can't we at least shake hands?'

Jesse held his out and waited. He was free, but he wanted to start the rest of his life without regrets. Tom hesitated for a fraction of a second, then took Jesse's hand in a firm grip. 'Yeah, sure.' In a slightly more gruff tone of voice he added, 'I meant what I said, have a nice life. Maybe I'll see you around.'

'Yeah, maybe you will.'

Jesse left before sadness overwhelmed him and he didn't look back. He drove his car over to Rain's house as fast as he could and ran up the steps to the door feeling almost lightheaded. He was free at last, and now Tom had admitted the truth, he could tell the world if he wanted. There was only one person he wanted to share his secret with for now though. And the minute she opened the door, he poured out the whole story to her, grinning from ear to ear. She smiled back, letting him talk until he ran out of steam. Then she wrapped her arms round his neck and kissed him.

'Rick Linden? Wow, that's wonderful, Jesse! I guess now

we know where you got your talent from, huh? Happy birthday, by the way,' she said.

'Oh, yeah, happy birthday to you too. Sorry, I should've said that first.'

'No, it's okay, I'm glad you've finally got some answers. Maybe that was the best present Tom Devlin could give you?'

'Yeah, for sure. I mean, I knew already, but it's such a relief to have it out in the open and not festering between us any longer.'

'Will you try and get in touch with Rick Linden, do you think?'

'Nah, he probably wouldn't want to know. But maybe if our band gets famous too, I'll write to him. He might be amused to find he's got a son who's following in his footsteps. And then he'd know I wasn't telling him just to scrounge off him. I don't want anything from him other than maybe an acknowledgement.'

Rain nodded. 'That sounds like a good plan. We'd better hurry up and write some more songs, then.'

'Definitely. But not today, we have some celebrating to do. Speaking of presents ...' He pulled out a small parcel from his pocket. 'Here's something for the birthday girl.'

'Oh, you shouldn't have! You need your money for other things.'

'Of course I should. I wanted to get you something to always remind you of me.' She opened the present and found a gold chain inside with a small gold charm in the shape of a pine cone. 'So you remember our night in the forest,' he said, and kissed her again.

'Thank you, it's lovely, absolutely perfect. Will you help me put it on, please?' He did and then she smiled at him mischievously. 'Actually, I've got a surprise for you too. Want to see it now?'

'Sure.'

'Okay, this way.'

As he followed her through the hallway and out the back door, he noticed for the first time that she was all dressed up in a beautiful short black dress that sparkled as she walked. Her arms were bare, despite the cold, and her dragon tattoo fit perfectly with her outfit.

'So you finally showed your Mom, huh?' He nodded at the dragon.

'Yes, and she did go ape, just as you predicted. Well, I knew she would too, but it's not as if I can get rid of it now, so she just kind of sighs every time she looks at it. I don't think she'll ever like it, but hey, it's my body.' Rain laughed. 'My dad thinks it's cool though. He told me when Mum wasn't listening.'

Jesse smiled at that. Her dad was a nice guy, but he liked her mom too. He wished he'd thought to dress up today, but knew that Rain's parents wouldn't mind. They accepted him the way he was and always seemed happy to see him.

When he and Rain emerged into the courtyard behind the house, her parents were standing there as if they'd been waiting for them. 'Happy birthday, dear boy,' they both said. Rowena gave him a hug, while Anthony shook his hand. 'Mind if we tag along?'

'No. I've no idea where we're going though.' Jesse was confused but continued to follow Rain. She went over to the huge garage on the other side of the courtyard and led the way up an outside staircase to the floor above. 'In here,' she said and went in, turning on the light. 'Ta-dah!' She held out a hand to indicate the space beyond. 'Do you like it?'

'What?' Jesse stared around him and saw a large room with a kitchenette, a small bedroom and a bathroom leading off it at one end. It all looked freshly painted and refurbished and the leather sofa in the first room smelled new.

'This is for you,' Rain said with a huge smile. 'Your new pad, if you want it? Mum and Dad say you can stay here for as long as you like. Until we finish high school and go on tour with Escape From Hell. And afterwards too, of course.'

'Rent free, naturally,' added Anthony. 'That's our birthday present to you.'

'I ... wow! Thank you. Really, I don't know what to say.' Jesse found himself almost speechless and the others laughed.

'It's a bit small,' Rowena said, 'but Rain didn't think you would mind. Will you be all right here, do you think?'

Jesse went over to give her a bear hug. 'I'll be more than all right, I'll be absolutely great. Thank you so much. You have no idea how much I appreciate it.'

'Well, it was either that or letting you move in with Rain, since you two seem to be practically welded together,' Anthony laughed. 'And we thought her room might start to feel a bit cramped after a while.'

Rain saw Jesse's astonishment and came to his rescue. 'Dad's just joking. Although you could've had a room for yourself in the house, I figured you'd prefer your own domain. Was I right?'

'Totally. You're all the best.'

'Right, well that's that sorted out, then,' Rowena said, sounding very satisfied. 'Now I expect you're hungry, but Rain has just one more tiny surprise for you, if you can bear to wait a bit longer?'

'Another one? No, come on, this is more than enough.' Jesse was starting to feel embarrassed. He wasn't used to receiving things.

'Well, this one's partly for me too, but you'll see. Let's go.'

Together the four of them trooped outside again and crossed the courtyard one more time, although not heading in the direction of the house. Instead, Rain took his hand and towed him over to a huge old barn that was standing a bit further away. Jesse had noticed it before, but never been in there. It looked a bit run-down, but when she pushed one of the big double doors open, it slid smoothly on oiled hinges. It was almost pitch dark in the barn, but the moment they stepped inside, it was as if all hell broke loose.

Lights came on, one after the other, music started blaring, and a huge video screen at one end of the vast room lit up. On it a film started showing the gig Escape From Hell had played at Northbrooke High. Jesse blinked and took in the fact that practically the entire Junior and Senior classes from school were inside the barn, all dressed up and shouting 'HAPPY BIRTHDAY, Rain and Jesse'. He spotted Zane and Mick, grinning at him, and a whole bunch of other well-known faces.

There were helium balloons floating everywhere, streamers and party poppers, and a table groaning with food, including a huge birthday cake. Jesse laughed out loud. 'Oh. My. God. This is crazy!'

'Are you ready to party?' Rain asked, shouting now to be heard over the noise everyone else was making. 'I told you we'd celebrate together if I was still here on November twenty-fourth.'

He grabbed her waist and lifted her up for a kiss, then swung her around. 'I'll party with you any time. This is just awesome, I love it!'

'Are you sure? I was afraid you might not want a party, but I did so here we are.'

'You know that whatever you want, I want. This is the best birthday I ever had, I swear.'

'Me too, because I'm sharing it with you. Let's go dance!'

He grabbed her hand and headed for the dance floor, where he wrapped her in his arms and buried his face in her hair. 'Have I told you lately that I totally adore you?'

'Maybe, but I'll never tire of hearing that because I love you just as much.'

'That's good, because I'm going to keep saying it for the rest of your life.'

Interview with Christina

Q **What inspired you to write *New England Rocks*?**

As I say in the Acknowledgements, I went to a high school reunion a couple of years ago and that made me think back nostalgically. But although I had a great time in high school, it could have been even better (especially in the boyfriend department!) and so that got me thinking about how I would have liked it to be and the kind of guy I would have liked to have met and dated. That turned into NER, a sort of daydream or wishful thinking I guess you could say.

Q ***New England Rocks* is the first part in a trilogy. What are your plans for the rest of the series?**

Well, the next book (*New England Crush*) will feature Rain's little sister Raven. Having heard all about what an awesome time Rain is having in the US, she decides to follow in her footsteps. But Raven is a completely different kind of girl so her experiences are not at all the same. Book three will feature another English girl, Sir Anthony's god-daughter Keri, plus a hero who has a small role in book two. After that, we will see!

Q **Jesse's cool rock band *Escape from Hell* plays a big part in the novel. What is your favourite rock band and why?**

At the moment I'm loving *Fall Out Boy*'s new album and I like most things by *All Time Low* and *My Chemical Romance*. I think because they have really catchy songs with a great chorus that make my feet tap :-) I'm also into more heavy metal stuff like *Korn* and *Linkin Park*, plus some of the old-style rock as well. My all time favourite will always be *Def Leppard* (I know, very 80s, but they wrote some awesome songs!)

About the Author

Christina Courtenay lives in Herefordshire and is married with two children. Although born in England she has a Swedish mother and was brought up in Sweden. In her teens, the family moved to Japan where she had the opportunity to travel extensively in the Far East.

Christina is chairman of the Romantic Novelists' Association. In 2011, Christina's first novel *Trade Winds* was short listed for The Romantic Novelists' Association's Award for Best Historical Fiction. Her second novel, *The Scarlet Kimono*, won the Big Red Reads' Best Historical Fiction Award. In 2012, *Highland Storms* won the RoNA for Best Historical Romantic Novel of the year. And *The Silent Touch of Shadows*, Christina's fourth novel, won the award for Best Historical Read at the Festival of Romance.

www.christinacourtenay.com
www.twitter.com/PiaCCourtenay
www.facebook.com/christinacourtenayauthor

More Choc Lit

From Christina Courtenay

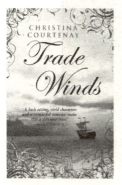

Trade Winds

Marriage of convenience or a love for life?

It's 1732 in Gothenburg, Sweden, and strong-willed Jess van Sandt knows only too well that it's a man's world. She believes she's being swindled out of her inheritance by her stepfather – and she's determined to stop it.

Short-listed for the Romantic Novelists' Association's Pure Passion Award for Best Historical Fiction 2011

Highland Storms

Who can you trust?

Betrayed by his brother and his childhood love, Brice Kinross needs a fresh start. So he welcomes the opportunity to leave Sweden for the Scottish Highlands to take over the family estate.

But there's trouble afoot at Rosyth in 1754 and Brice finds himself unwelcome. The estate's in ruin and money is disappearing. He discovers an ally in Marsaili Buchanan, the beautiful redheaded housekeeper, but can he trust her?

Winner of the 2012 Best Historical Romantic Novel of the year

Sequel to Trade Winds

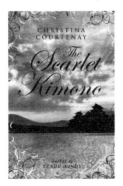

The Scarlet Kimono

Abducted by a Samurai warlord in 17th-century Japan – what happens when fear turns to love?

England, 1611, and young Hannah Marston envies her brother's adventurous life. But when she stows away on his merchant ship, her powers of endurance are stretched to their limit. Then they reach Japan and all her suffering seems worthwhile – until she is abducted by Taro Kumashiro's warriors.

Winner of the 2011 Big Red Read's Best Historical Fiction Award

The Gilded Fan

How do you start a new life, leaving behind all you love?

It's 1641, and when Midori Kumashiro, the orphaned daughter of a warlord, is told she has to leave Japan or die, she has no choice but to flee to England. Midori is trained in the arts of war, but is that enough to help her survive a journey, with a lecherous crew and an attractive captain she doesn't trust?

Sequel to The Scarlet Kimono

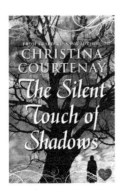

The Silent Touch of Shadows

What will it take to put the past to rest?

Professional genealogist Melissa Grantham receives an invitation to visit her family's ancestral home, Ashleigh Manor. From the moment she arrives, life-like dreams and visions haunt her. The spiritual connection to a medieval young woman and her forbidden lover have her questioning her sanity, but Melissa is determined to solve the mystery.

A haunting love story set partly in the present and partly in fifteenth century Kent.

Winner of the 2012 Best Historical Read from the Festival of Romance

More from Choc Lit

If you loved Christina's story,
you'll enjoy the rest of our selection:

Visit www.choc-lit.com for more details
including the first two chapters and reviews

Introducing *Choc Lit*

We're an independent publisher creating
a delicious selection of fiction.
Where heroes are like chocolate – irresistible!
Quality stories with a romance at the heart.

Choc Lit novels are selected by genuine readers like yourself.
We only publish stories our Choc Lit Tasting Panel want to
see in print. Our reviews and awards speak for themselves.

Come and support our authors and join them in our
Author's Corner, read their interviews and see their latest
events, reviews and gossip.

Visit: www.choc-lit.com for more details.

Available in paperback and as ebooks from most stores.

We'd also love to hear how you enjoyed *New England Rocks*.
Just visit www.choc-lit.com and give your feedback.
Describe Jesse in terms of chocolate
and you could win a Choc Lit novel in our
Flavour of the Month competition.

Follow us on twitter: www.twitter.com/ChocLituk and
facebook: www.facebook.com/pages/Choc-Lit/30680012481,
or simply scan barcode using your mobile phone QR reader:

Twitter   *Facebook*